The Rice Filter

By Kenton Samuels

The Rice Filter
Published 2013
ISBN 978-1-482-62455-7

Also available in hardback, published 2013
and in e-book format, published 2012

ACKNOWLEDGEMENT
Mark Twain quote from his letter to William T. Stead,
9th January 1899

CHAPTERS

Peace by persuasion has a pleasant sound, but I think we should not be able to work it. We should have to tame the human race first, and history seems to show that that cannot be done.
– Mark Twain

1
Mr. Nishi is Probably Unhappy With Me.

Twenty minutes ago, the world was perfect. Twenty minutes ago, I'd spent five and a half years processing births, deaths and marriages at the DBDM, I'd been a slightly uncomfortable witness to one birth, I'd been fortunate enough to have never seen a dead body and I'd been a semi-anonymous guest at two weddings: this was perfection. Well, perfect for me; just the right balance of experience and anonymity nicely wrapped up in a sense of having been reasonably useful. I wish I could go back twenty minutes and fully embrace perfection but I can't. The dead body is very much in the way of that.

I'm not certain whether or not I intended to kill him. I think it was more like a reflex, like a 'him or me' moment. It's quite hard to remember exactly.

Something tight is spreading from my chest. I think it might be panic, I'm not sure. I hope it's not something serious. It's emulating the patch of red spreading from near the centre of the dead man's chest. What's his name again? Sorry, what *was* his name again? Mr. Nishi, that's it. It's like he deliberately put on a super-clean shirt this morning just to emphasize the contrast between his pristine white office wear and the vibrant blood he somehow knew he was going to shed today. This is another reason not to like him.

My heart is racing, it's pumping so hard it's starting to hurt. I wonder if I'm having a heart attack. Maybe that's the feeling spreading out from my chest; maybe that's my punishment for shooting him: a heart attack. I guess it would serve me right.

It's difficult to breathe now too. I roll myself off Mr. Nishi onto the ground beside him and lay as still as a corpse myself, staring at the cloudless blue sky beyond the walls of the side street, listening to the frantic thudding in my chest. I want to scream but the sound is stuck in my throat and my mouth locks open. I'm literally dumbstruck. I didn't even know that the word was based on an actual phenomenon. A few moments pass before I'm sure that it isn't a heart attack, that it is just panic. Eventually, after I don't know how long, I stand up; there's still no one around. And I realise I'm still holding onto the gun. I go to throw it aside, but a surprising thought stops me: *'My traces are on this!'* What do I do now? There's a clean handkerchief in my pocket and a tube of hand cleansing gel in my briefcase. Had I not been so preoccupied this morning with thoughts of goodbyes and reunions and of leaving the city I love, I would have been thinking more about the incredible heat today and I would have used the handkerchief to wipe the sweat from my face. Because it hasn't been used, it and the gel will be perfect to wipe any evidence of my presence from the gun, surely. But if I do that, won't it be a calculated action? Up until this point, this whole nightmare has been an accident if I remember correctly. Maybe manslaughter at worst. If I wipe the gun, there will be no denying that I'm attempting to get away with it. But what else can I do? Own up to it and hope for the best? What can I possibly hope for? For the police to offer a kind listening ear? For the Harvest to ignore this misdemeanour? Not likely. I need to think. I need *time* to think. There must be something I can do. I pull out my handkerchief and take the tube from my briefcase, I squeeze some gel into the handkerchief, and I wipe down the handle, the trigger and the barrel of the gun, and drop it beside Mr. Nishi. I'm hardly able to look at him.

Now there's another feeling with my panic: guilt. '*What have I done? This is a man, a person, a real human being like me. What am I doing?*' But guilt will have to wait for a moment: I've just seen my discarded phone on the ground and now I remember my watch in Mr. Nishi's pocket. I have to retrieve them. If I leave any of my belongings here, the police will have no trouble tracing the crime straight to me. Tears almost come to my eyes as I dig my hand into the dead man's pocket and fish out my watch. There's nothing else in there and I'm strangely relieved at that – I don't know why. It disturbs me that he's still warm but of course he is: it's a tremendously hot day and I've only just killed him.

I have to clear my mind, I have to think about what to do next. Wiping the gun, retrieving my belongings, all of this is necessary. '*Necessary for what? For me to escape? To cover up what I've done? Am I some kind of monster?*' I curse myself and pick up the phone, suddenly noticing splashes of blood on my shirt and tie. A feeble whimper escapes from me and I involuntarily shed a few tears. There isn't a great deal of blood on my clothes but my attempts to rub it away prove futile, only smearing what's there, making it look worse. If I put my suit jacket back on and fasten the buttons, it will certainly hide the stains but then I'll be in danger of heat stroke. The temperature control in my jacket hasn't been working for over a month but I've put off getting it fixed or buying a new jacket because they're always more expensive in the summer. I'm such an idiot. But there's no choice; I put the jacket back on, button it up, dab my eyes with a dry corner of the handkerchief, and try to calm myself down. I'm already starting to boil in the heat but I have to try and ignore it. I close my eyes, I inhale, hold my breath for two seconds, and breathe out through the mouth; I rub the back of my neck and I imagine a calm lake and endless green forests, somewhere completely devoid of people and death. It's a nice enough scene but it's not very helpful, and I can't do this for very long. I need to think; I'll continue on to the office, I can still make it in time, I'll be able to focus better there.

As I walk away, something makes me turn and look at Mr. Nishi's body, like somehow I owe him this courtesy. He looks smaller now, a little less detailed, a little less dead maybe, but he is still dead and I've still killed him. How has this happened? It can't be real! I start to cry again. "I'm so sorry," I mumble to him.

I don't think he cares that I'm sorry.

2
The Four Days of Harvest.

Back in the perfect world, I had no idea that things were actually perfect. If I'd known, maybe I would've been laughing and dancing and hugging the strangers on the monorail on my way to work. Or maybe I wouldn't. In fact, I know I wouldn't, but maybe I should have. Instead I was trying hard not to think about the fourth thing.

All of us are trained to remember the fourth thing: every person on the monorail this morning, every citizen in this entire megatropolis, and up until recently, Mr. Nishi too; we just don't realise we've been trained to remember it. Actually, it would be more precise to say we don't realise we've been trained to remember *them*: *they* are the four important things. They're not taught in the classroom, at least not in the way mathematics or science is taught. We don't write out formulae or sit exams for them; they're not downloaded to a little pocket book and given to every man, woman and child to memorise. We've been trained to remember them the same way we've been trained to remember that the sun rises and sets, that gravity anchors us to the Earth, that we must eat and drink in order to live: observation, experience and understanding. It's hard not to think about them because even when we're not doing so consciously, they're always there. The four important things make up the world and who we are in it, but giving them a grandiose title like *The Four Principal Knowledges* or *The Four Great Absolutes* would be pointless. It would be like giving the title, *The Great and Noble In- and Exhalation*, to the act of breathing.

The first important thing we're trained to remember is that we're only here in the city for a relatively short time. This is only a temporary place to live, just until we're old enough, or mature enough, or fully-rounded enough as individuals to move on. To be honest, I have absolutely no idea of the real criteria for determining when we leave, and I'll bet no one else knows either. Maybe it really is to do with age or maturity, maybe it's to do with something nobody's thought of yet. The four important things are four important *basics*: the details seem to have been left up to scholars to discuss and everyone else to argue about. As far as I'm aware, the only point we all agree on with the first important thing, is that once we've reached eighteen years old, we're just as likely as the next person to be minding our own business one moment and a possible candidate for Harvest the next. Harvest Week comes once every seven years and this diary event is the second important thing we remember. The week begins with Harvestee Day when the names of one thousand citizens (designated 'Harvestees') are announced, followed by six days of holiday and preparation (though for some reason, only four days if you work for the DBDM), culminating in Harvest Day when the Harvest Light comes to teleport the one thousand Harvestees out of the city to their new homes. The third important thing is that although the Harvest process may appear frightening, it really shouldn't be feared, provided we've kept the law and haven't done wrong. The fourth and most important thing we're trained to remember is simply not to do wrong.

I'd been trying very hard not to think about the fourth thing but riding the monorail to work today gave me plenty of time to do just that. If it had been any other day, I would have been standing in that same spot in the middle of the carriage, thinking about mundane things; things to do with my job in the civil service or other blissfully inconsequential matters. I would have been questioning my growing reliance on setting the Meal Make to 'Surprise Me' and considering whether or not I should cook something for dinner myself. I'd have been contemplating whether to grow a beard or not, and if I do, artistic goatee or charismatic short-trim? I've been through this particular discussion with myself more times than I have on maybe any other subject. I'm not sure why. I wouldn't necessarily be trying to impress anyone with the beard but it seems most women and even some men tend not to understand how difficult a thing it can be to grow facial hair that doesn't look somehow wrong. Maybe now that I've hit thirty-four, I should try again. Or I could. I doubt I'll be thinking about it much now, what with having just killed somebody. The Harvest Light isn't going to reconsider my guilty stance on account of me having a rather fetching beard. Anyway, just occasionally in all of this mental housekeeping, the fourth important thing would consciously cross my mind as a semi-friendly nudge to keep me in check. But today is my final day at work and rather than thinking about the happy period of free days I was soon to have or the work colleagues I might miss, the fourth thing was all I could think about. With hindsight, I'm sure I hadn't done many things wrong, but they all pale into nothing now, compared to this. Maybe my concerns were prophetic. I certainly wish I'd seen this coming.

I resume my journey to work, hurrying my steps as I go but trying not to look like I'm hurrying. A running man draws attention to himself. A running man with a broken temperature control jacket collapsing from heat exhaustion draws even more. I can't get back on the monorail because standing in extreme close quarters with a multitude of bored strangers, what if one of them sees down my jacket to the blood I'm trying to hide? What if there's more in plain sight that I've missed? I can't risk exposure until I've thought about my options. Walking should be useful, it should give me time to focus my thoughts. At least that's the plan. Instead, all I can do as I hurry along is lament the perfect world that's now passed and try to reason why the nightmare I'm living now is. I'm Nicholas Machida, I'm thirty-four, I'm a processor in the Department for Births, Deaths and Marriages, commonly referred to as the DBDM. This has been my ambition since college – really. Most of my university friends wanted media fame or business success, but there's an inherent, confidential air of trust bestowed upon DBDM employees, an unspoken solemn respect for the work we do, and that's all I ever craved: to be appreciated but without the unwanted attention. I've achieved my ambition, I should have been happy. But in that perfect world where I'd killed no one, I still didn't feel fulfilled, and bizarrely, it was in part down to the very job I was so happy to be in: processing all of those marriages was a constant reminder that I'm not married.

There's a girl I'm engaged to – I've been so for seven years – and I miss her terribly. I wish she were here now. I can only put it down to sheer, incalculable bad luck that only a few days after our engagement, it was announced that my fiancé, Naomi, the kindest, most beautiful girl I've ever known (yes, I'm biased), was to be a Harvestee. And then six awful days after the notification, she was taken. Harvest Week is supposed to be a special time: an event transcending our trifling cares and concerns by its sheer enormity and importance. But that particular Harvest was awful, even worse than the Harvest seven years before when my parents went away. I missed my parents obviously, but when Naomi went, I remember feeling that I wasn't up to the task of continuing a normal life without her. And in a way, I haven't. I feel like I've been merely surviving. For more than fifteen years before we even began discussing marriage, Naomi and I had been the closest of friends; we had no secrets from each other. It only took so long to get to the point of marriage because we initially feared the shift in the relationship might somehow damage our friendship. But the more years we spent together, the closer we grew, and the more I realised that the complete abandonment and simultaneous fulfilment of self that I was feeling through Naomi was in fact love. It was also something of a massive bonus that she'd developed the same way toward me. Our marriage was certain. Of course, all of those years of friendship only served to make the timing of her departure all the more difficult, and I still ask myself every day why I took so long to act. I've just never been one to rush into things, I suppose. Still, as hard as that time was, at least I had good friends around me and an overly busy pre-DBDM job to keep me occupied. *'Thank you, other best friend Esther, and thank you, Shimamoto Unlimited Communications. You're the best!'* And in all of the time we've been apart, I don't believe I've ever even looked at another woman romantically because I'm confident Naomi's still waiting for me. It's not that I'm surprised at my self-control, I'm just impressed.

That's mostly trivial now, considering what I've done. Mr. Nishi won't be able to experience love now, he won't be able to lose himself in the busyness of work, he won't feel the benefit of having good friends around him. I'm filled with an awful dread as it dawns on me that I might have left a wife without a husband or children without a father. I am a monster. But do monsters feel? Do they take time to consider other people? Do they have human pasts that are as important to them now as they were then? I still do. That must count for something, humanity-wise. When the time came for Naomi to go, it was fairly obvious to me and to everyone else that the Harvest would take her to the city of Euchaea – the best possible outcome. I have no proof of this, of course; there's no real way to prove these things one way or the other. Still, with Naomi, Euchaea would be a very safe bet. Even if I didn't have my biases, I still think she fits the criteria for maturity and whatever else might be necessary to go there, no problem. That being the case, after her Harvest announcement, rather than rushing a wedding ceremony in the six days we had left together, we postponed the wedding until I could join her. It was a reasonably safe assumption that if Naomi were in that Harvest but I wasn't, I'd be in the next one. Then we'd be able to have the kind of big ceremony she really wanted. Like the notion of Naomi going to Euchaea, there was no particular proof to back up the idea that I'd be in the next Harvest either, but that's the key to understanding how the world works, or at least the key to *accepting* how it works: somehow our *Rice Grains* would simply know of our connection, ergo it would be only natural for the next Harvest to call me. To say I was feeling incredibly excited twenty minutes ago – now I guess maybe twenty-five or thirty minutes ago – is an understatement: the next Harvest is only four days away and I have indeed been called! And that's also why I couldn't stop thinking about the fourth thing.

3
The Matters and Mechanisms of Perfection.

I never asked my parents what the Rice Grain was. I never asked anyone; there was no need. It's like the four important things: no one needs to ask about them because we grow up knowing them: they just *are*. And the Rice Grain just *is*. But it's a more tangible *is*. We all have a Rice Grain. In some of us, it sits somewhere toward the front of the brain, sandwiched between the left and right hemispheres, and in the rest of us, it's fused to the brainstem. I sometimes used to spend my morning monorail journeys trying to guess where the other passengers' Rice Grains were. Some people claim the location of a person's Grain can affect personality and manifest itself in certain characteristics: people who's Grain sits between the hemispheres (H-Types) are said to be more inclined toward extroversion but are secretly thoughtful about it, while people with their Grain on their brainstem (S-Types) are allegedly introverted and rational but constantly struggling with impatience. That would suggest that most of the people I've ever met are S-Types, so I don't think it's necessarily true. That being said, I am an S-Type, so at least some of the ideas fit. But wherever our Rice Grains are, H-Type or S-Type, there's no way to survive without it; not having a Rice Grain would be like not having a heart or a brain: we'd simply be unable to function. The Rice Grain is the most important element of the Harvest. In appearance, it's nothing more than a tiny piece of hard grey carbon – "complex-carbon", they call it – but in truth, it's the most sophisticated bio-computer ever built and the only item ever to transcend both the terms "technological marvel" and "supernatural wonder". One of its roles is to coordinate our bodies' first-response medical nanobots if we break a bone or catch a cold or contract something serious; I've lost count of the amount of stories I've heard of accident victims or people on the verge of death being narrowly sustained by the resourceful little workers until full medical help arrived, and even once of the Grain directing a host's nanobots to cause the person to vomit up an accidentally ingested poison when it recognised a chemical trace that the host had known nothing about. I'm not sure if this one's just an urban myth, but it certainly sounds like something the Grain and the nanobots could conceivably manage. But there's far more to the Rice Grain than that. Its primary function is to record and store our personal data, which may not sound so significant, but in this city, such information is as important as life itself. Some go so far as to say it *is* life itself.

Called a Rice Grain because of the similarity in size and shape of the original Grains, many centuries ago, to a rice grain of the food variety (though they're now a fraction of that size), the original Rice Grains were administered to women as soon as they became pregnant and absorbed into the forming embryos some time during the first three months of development. Apparently, it had never been a design specification for the Grain to place itself only between the hemispheres or on the brainstem, but that was the way it always happened, and to this day the reason for this bizarre migration remains one of life's mysteries.

The aim of the Rice Grain, the recording and storing of our ever-accumulating data, hasn't changed since the beginning, but we have. We're told it all started out quite innocently. The Rice Grain facilitated an efficient means of statistical analysis, automatically logging civic information such as employment details and residential addresses, right through from the moment of birth to the moment of death. Perhaps that's why so much respect is afforded to the DBDM: because we work so closely with the Rice Grain. Anyhow, maybe this is just me but it's obvious that recording these details wasn't going to amount to the full extent of the Rice Grain's use. Capability inspired possibility and the Grain's role quickly grew to include uses for shopping and banking, medical tracking and care, city services registration, even optional relationship matching, and just about everything else required to keep any megatropolis or well-organised country running smoothly and its citizens reasonably happy. From its relatively humble beginnings, the Rice Grain became essential. The more we used it, the more we found uses for it, and the more our bodies became accustomed to interacting with it. The following centuries saw interaction become integration, so much so that over the course of several generations, it was discovered (I'm sure to the absolute horror of many at the time) that the human body had grown so reliant on this integration with the little biological computer that the Rice Grain had started to form 'naturally' in embryos as they took shape. Every analysis showed these naturally occurring Rice Grains to be completely identical to the artificial Rice Grains in every way, right down to their hard complex-carbon molecular structure, the bio-algorithmic sequences used to store personal information, and even their smooth rice grain shape. And still they only formed on the brainstem or between the brain's hemispheres.

The true gravity and importance of the Rice Grain, however (and the reason why it's more than just a feeling of guilt I'm struggling with now), was still to come and this is tied directly to the first important thing we must remember: this city is only a temporary place in which to live. The perfect world before I killed Mr. Nishi was good; it was mostly clean, comfortable and well-organised. My old middle school history teacher, Mr. Oto, wouldn't have called it perfect, but he never called anything perfect, not even Euchaea. Even with the great City itself, he only went so far as to call it "close to perfect". He always liked to stress humanity's fallibility and said more times than I can remember that as soon as human beings became involved in any equation, faults, however slight, were inevitable. He also made a point of telling us time and time again about the human cost of the endeavour toward the so-called perfect Euchaea, affirming and reaffirming that to reach that stage of near-perfection took centuries of mostly disastrous trial and error. A variety of outlandish and morally ambiguous ideas were explored, from vast brainwashing programs to selective cloning to cultivating entire populations oblivious to the potential horrors of the human condition. No suggestion was apparently out of bounds or not worth a try to reach this most justified of goals: outright oppression through fear and punishment, terror and dictatorship, even extremely friendly coercion. We soon saw that humanity's ultimately good intentions were more often than not, punctuated with a collapse of governments or a civil war, or sometimes both, and Mr. Oto was forever there to tell us just how bad it was. He always came across as an unhappy man being forced to teach us history as a punishment for some crime he'd committed and his obvious lack of faith in the human race found expression in his lessons. I don't think he managed to completely instil this attitude in his students but sometimes I look at my own pessimism and certainly the human disaster I'm in now and I'm almost certain I can trace it back to him. He also had a beard, which in an odd way deters me from growing one. If I ever decide to go ahead, I'll make sure mine differs from his. I think I'm leaning toward artistic goatee.

'What the hell am I thinking?' Growing a beard? I've just shot and killed a man and now I'm walking to work with his blood on my shirt, trying to pretend that nothing's happened. Why am I thinking about beards? What's the matter with me? Maybe Mr. Oto was right: humans are accidents waiting to happen, volatile components waiting to explode. He never said this outright but maybe he just wasn't allowed to as a teacher.

It's strange that after all of those controversial, complicated and disastrous efforts to create Euchaea, it was the very uncomplicated idea of a filter system, designed to remove the more unsavoury people from society that eventually became what's in place now. Or maybe I only think it's strange because Mr. Oto always said it was. After everything that had already been tried, I think he found the final solution to be a little too simple. Of course, the idea in its more developed form couldn't have undesirable citizens plucked away from the city if found guilty of a crime: this would do nothing to prevent crimes from being committed in the first place. Hardly a perfect society. Instead the filter was effectively reversed and the whole process done in stages: we are born and raised in what is, in effect, the *nursery* city, a record of our birth and family particulars, education, employment, transactions, medical status, psychological profile, are stored and updated on the Rice Grain, and every seven years on Harvest Day when the one thousand Harvestees are removed from the city by the Harvest Light, it's the information on the Rice Grain that the Light reads. The Light itself – a great wall of amber light five metres deep and stretching right across the city and upward into the heavens – makes a solitary pass from one end of the city to the other and there's no escaping it; many have tried: hiding in sealed rooms, under ground, in the air; but the Light penetrates everything. It moves at precisely 2.01 metres per second, "The optimum speed for ominous effect", people say, and they say it for good reason. It's a strange and terrifying sight that constantly defies comprehension. Even the third important thing we remember, the encouragement not to fear the Harvest process, rings somewhat hollow on Harvest Day. And as the Light reads the Harvestees' Rice Grains, those it finds 'suitable' or 'appropriate' are teleported to Euchaea to live and work in the best city mankind has ever managed to produce. There lies the perfect society. Or the close to perfect society, according to Mr. Oto.

Teleporting the one thousand Harvestees out of the city isn't the end of the matter however: not every person to go through the filter is deemed fit to inhabit Euchaea. There has to be a third city. Designed primarily for holding the truly apathetic, the lawless, and the most despicable of society – all of the people the filter rejects – it's the very worst of places, a mass prison without law, privilege or parole, and afforded no ties or support from the governing bodies over Euchaea or our own city. Indeed, as it's where all of the filter refuse is held, it's essentially forgotten, like it doesn't exist. Some refer to that city as "The Third" or "The Terror" but the truth is, the place is so disregarded, it doesn't even have a name.

If it wasn't for 'The Scrutiny of Harold Kanagawa', none of this would matter to me at all.

4
A Change In The Law of Nature.

Of all of the important people I've never met, Harold Kanagawa is probably the one to whom I owe the most thanks and the most hatred. He has literally been an example to all of us, a real person turned into a cautionary tale for generations of children and adults alike, of what can happen to you when you don't take the four important things seriously. The incident that came to be known as 'The Scrutiny of Harold Kanagawa' occurred hundreds of years ago at the first ever Harvest but it's still cited today. Mr. Kanagawa, an extremely high-standing bank manager and minor media personality of his day, had for many years been very craftily siphoning money from his own bank to help cover the costs of his and his wife's expensive tastes, and those of his mistress. Aside from that, he'd lived a reasonably respectable life. When his Harvest came (the day after the first and following six Harvests, names and *destinations* were published), it was revealed that rather than going to Euchaea as everyone had expected, Mr. Kanagawa had instead gone to the other city. Initially, it was all thought to be a catastrophic error, some malfunction in the Rice Grain or the amber light, and the entire Harvest was called into question. However, thorough investigations and a degree of luck on the part of the police eventually uncovered Kanagawa's crime. Not only that, he was also found to have carefully planned (though not carried out) the murder of his wife and a senior police official, and paid a gangster to force the resignation of a rival employee, helping to facilitate his rise to bank manager. The crimes weren't in any way related;

no one had known about them except Kanagawa himself and the gangster, who'd since died in a gangland shooting; not even Kanagawa's wife or mistress knew about the stolen money and they certainly had no idea about the murder plot. However, at Kanagawa's final appeal hearing (he had fifteen in all), a forced examination of his classified Rice Grain readings revealed that the Grain had gone far beyond recording mere physical data. As far as the analysts were able to tell, it seemed a record of every memory, every emotion, literally an account of Kanagawa's entire life, including every secret crime and every secret feeling, had been stored on the tiny Grain and processed by the Harvest's amber light. The Rice Grain and the Harvest Light were *intelligent* beyond their design. There was no question they would continue. Inevitably, there were decades of protests, peaceful and violent, and even the rising and falling of two political parties a couple of generations apart basing their central policies on 'the unpredictability and, therefore, the injustice and atrocity of the Harvest'. The protests and anti-Harvest policies were relatively short-lived: the only thing the unforeseen events of Harold Kanagawa proved was that the Grain and the Harvest were efficient and effective, only somehow in a form purer than anyone could have imagined. And Kanagawa's was not the only case in which someone expected to go to Euchaea but failed to be admitted, or indeed where someone *didn't* expect to go to Euchaea but succeeded; hundreds of others in that first Harvest and every Harvest since, were revealed to have similar hidden, almost untraceable crimes, preventing their favourable move, or shown to be innocent of some crime they were branded with in the city. Even to this day, and with still on-going research, quite how the Rice Grain records such thorough yet intangible detail, not one person can answer. I thank Mr.

Kanagawa because for thirty-four years, his grave errors constantly in the back of my mind have helped keep me from straying into bad territory. I hate him because due to those same errors, I'm now no longer blissfully unaware of the horror that could be awaiting me.

My Rice Grain probably knows that it was 37.8 degrees at about the time when Mr. Nishi died and that I'd first thought it was about 38.5 degrees. I'd looked at the temperature display above the monorail door because the heat was starting to get to me despite the carriage providing air conditioning for passengers without environment-controlled clothing (or for those too miserly to have theirs fixed). It's like this every Harvest Week; a late-August sortie of blazing sunshine and barely tolerable humidity to shock us out of the three months of daily rain we've just endured. I should be used to it by now; before this horrible turn of events, I should have been enjoying it. I should have been laying on the grass in a park somewhere, absorbing the rays through a sensible shirt, thinking about all of the things I didn't have to do. This is my Harvest Week: I'm supposed to be free of responsibility, revelling in the simple fact of being alive, taking the time to appreciate everything that until now, the need to work has hindered. Instead, like most of the other passengers on the crowded monorail, I was in an office suit, stoically suffering under the heat and the responsibility and the reality of work and bills and of things not being the way I really wanted them to be, and I was trying to look like I was taking it all in my stride.

I took my suit jacket off because the crush of people was making me sweat. It was a small feat of physical dexterity to slip it off in the confined space available and thread it through the handle of my briefcase. As soon as I did so, the cooled air hit the damp patches under my armpits and on my back, and gave me such a shock that I let out an involuntary and extremely humiliating shriek. It snapped the man next to me out of his daydream and I started to sweat out of embarrassment rather than overheating. Impressively, he managed to avoid eye contact with me and briefly looked around the carriage, pretending it wasn't me who'd startled him, but we both knew. Soon he looked back to the floor and resumed his daydream and I gritted my teeth against the freezing cold.

At the time, it made me wonder if my Rice Grain was recording how uncomfortable I felt. When my Harvest came, would the Harvest Light have to process this little incident on top of everything else, like it processed every trivial little incident of Harold Kanagawa's life too? I was sure there was already enough to keep it occupied: my now insignificant concerns about past misdemeanours, my up and down emotional state since my Harvestee announcement two days ago; I suspected my Grain might even be getting worn out by all of the strain. (I knew this wasn't actually true; the Grain can't be worn out by anything). In times of stress, I often find myself rubbing the base of my skull and I was doing it again then; it always feels like I'm giving my Rice Grain a relaxing massage. I know this effect isn't actually true either, I can't massage my Grain, but the placebo always works. As I hurry along, I realise I'm doing it now too. It doesn't work anymore.

5

The Cost of A Red Roof and The Reason Why Crime Can Be A Good Thing.

The streets are unusually narrow here. It's like they're hiding me, aiding my 'escape' to work, but I know they're going to open up again soon. Soon I'll be back amongst the ground transports and the crowds, the mega-convenience stores, the ornate houses, the drab school buildings. I turn two more corners in quick succession, a right and a left, and suddenly I'm surrounded by familiarity again. Wide streets and tall, gleaming office buildings, wooden food stalls and re-painted shrines, slanting tiled roofs set against gentle glass arcs. I'm back where I should have been all along, where I should never have strayed from for the pointless sake of sentimentality.

It was another tiled roof, a red one, that triggered this whole thing off. Opposite my rather mundane apartment is an equally average-looking house with a red roof. However, the garden of that average-looking house is an exotic haven, a beautifully maintained display of amazing flowers, yellow and green, red and turquoise, leaves and shrubbery so pastel, they look like a shifting green-lilac-charcoal mist. Every morning I see the garden and it amazes me. It gives me the colour-infused energy I'm going to need for the rest of the day. The red roof is visible from the monorail carriage as it passes by and while I rode the monorail this morning, looking out at all of the uninteresting roofs and trying not to think about the fourth thing, it suddenly struck me that that was exactly what everyone else was doing too. Not one other person in the entire carriage knew about the amazing garden and the all-important energy it gave because all they saw was the red roof. I actually started to feel sorry for them, and then I started to feel sorry for myself. What stunning but hidden features of the city had I been missing because of my five and a half years of routine, seeing only dull roofs every day? I wouldn't usually care but this was to be my last journey to work before my Harvest. I needed to do something different, to see something special, today or never. I'd already made a half-hearted attempt at this, setting out to work a little earlier than usual, but it made no difference as I only ended up walking slower and catching the same monorail I usually do. But the inclination was there. Naomi would probably say I was being pedantic (in that cute faux-mockery way she does) and that I shouldn't over-analyse things, but it's a quality essential for a successful career in the DBDM. And besides, I prefer to think of it as trying to appreciate every detail. I was missing out; I was forfeiting the potential enjoyment of my surroundings for mundane routine and the sudden thought of this was giving me an uneasy feeling in the pit of my stomach. I couldn't tell what was happening to me; it didn't feel particularly good or bad, just odd. I fully expected Euchaea to be great, I was looking forward to it, but it didn't feel right just to dismiss this place, to not acknowledge and appreciate some previously unseen gem of a building or enigmatic piece of street art in that final daytime pass through the area. *Why?* Why didn't I feel it was okay to just ignore everything and leave? I wish so much that I had! Far too swiftly, my mind was made up to get off at the next stop and walk the rest of the way.

I even hesitated at the doors. As they slid open and the heat from outside hit me like the blast of a furnace, I reconsidered. I always reconsider. This is something Naomi isn't at all keen on. It pains me to know there's something about me that she doesn't love but she's always put up with it. I actually set myself the goal of becoming more decisive and assertive during our seven-year separation but I think I may have failed. Standing like a lost child at the open doors, I thought about the pros and cons of walking the rest of the way to work: the fresh air, the space, the potential to be pleasantly surprised by some architecture I hadn't seen before, the unappealing prospect of being soaked through with sweat before I even got to work, the physical tiredness I'd have to bear all morning, sun burn. But I'd decided to walk for a reason. None of that had changed so I set off.

Once I got to ground level, everything looked different. It wasn't just the fact that I hadn't physically set foot in that area before; it all seemed quite a big departure from 'normal': the little streets were virtually empty, I could see only two ground transports from where I stood, which was pretty much in the middle of the street, and the rest of the cars and buses flying along up in the sky lanes seemed so far away, further than I'd ever seen them. Even people seemed sparse. Near-empty streets at rush hour were something I'd somehow managed to miss in thirty-four years in the city. It was a strange experience, maybe even a little uncomfortable, but at the same time oddly liberating. I suddenly had a space to myself, somewhere other than my small apartment or my desk at work or my limited headspace on the monorail, where I could be away from the oppressive busyness of the crowds. I suddenly had precious extra time to think and reflect and over-analyse. I wished I'd walked to work more often.

As I walked and thought about the interesting old buildings I saw, I began to wonder what the architecture in Euchaea would be like. Would they have the same blend of traditional and ultra-modern there too? Would everything be new? Would it be some style I'd never even imagined before? Naomi would know. She'd been there seven years, she'd be accustomed to Euchaea's architecture. The graceful merging of old and new in the city she left behind would probably look strange to her now. I wondered if I'd look strange to her too. As is often the case, I was soon thinking again about all that could potentially change about us in our seven-year separation. I don't like to have these thoughts; I want to remember Naomi as she was, but I know I shouldn't. I know she's somehow different now, but not knowing in what way just makes everything harder. I started to question again why this was happening: why Naomi and I were in this situation of being separated? I wasn't questioning the necessity of the Harvest, but it did always make me wonder: if the Harvest Light and the Rice Grain really were so great, so far beyond our comprehension, if they really were able to know the un-knowable and baffle the most amazing human minds, why didn't they take Naomi and I together? The Harvest must have known of our engagement. I'm no genius, but surely common sense would have had the two of us sent to Euchaea at the same time, not seven whole years apart. It was then that I realised I had an opportunity with my Harvest being only four days away: if there was some kind of information bureau in Euchaea, I could make a point of asking that very question.

But then Mr. Nishi turned up. I was so absorbed in my thoughts about Naomi and the Harvest that it took me a moment to realise that the only other man around was staring at me and that he was in my way or I was in his. I mumbled something and bowed slightly to get by, but he raised his hand and held onto my shoulder. Immediately I knew this wasn't good. The man was possibly in his early forties; he was wearing a smart grey suit and a large smile. "Happy Harvest, citizen," he said. My tension didn't ease when he took his hand from my shoulder and bowed. I could tell he wasn't a *regular* member of the morning rush. I also realised I was standing with him in a window-less side street. How did I get there? *'Is this guy a salesman?'* I wondered, trying to see the most unthreatening reason for him to stop me. *'If so, he's not a very good one.'* "You'll have to excuse me," I said to him. "I have to go to work." He raised his hand again and I stepped back, a little more than I'd intend to. I'm sure he noticed.

"This'll only take a second," he said. "I just want to take something."

I wasn't certain I'd heard him correctly. I was hoping I hadn't. "Pardon?"

"Money, phone, anything you have."

It had all turned very unpleasant very quickly, but with the few wits I had left, I tried to use my confusion to my advantage by pretending I hadn't understood what was going on. *'If I ignore him, he's as good as not there,'* I thought, and I looked down at the ground and started walking again.

"Sorry, where the hell are you going?"

I couldn't help but stop and look up at the man again. His smile had dropped a little. And he was holding a handgun.

"I'm sure it's just the excitement of Harvest Week why you're walking away," he continued. "I understand entirely, you're not concentrating. Now please, hand something over."

My eyes locked on the gun and my hands shot up in the air, briefcase, jacket and all. The weapon was pointing right at my torso. Even if I'd had the speed and reflexes of a cheetah, I wouldn't have been able to move out of the way if he decided to pull the trigger. I couldn't understand how this was happening? I still can't. I was being mugged. Only a couple of days left in the city and I was being mugged. After thirty-four years! And why was there nobody around to alert the police? "I'm sorry! Yes, I wasn't thinking!" I stammered. "I have a watch. And a phone. Here, you can have them." My fingers fumbled over the buckle of my watchstrap as though it was the first time I'd ever tried to undo it. My coordination and my composure were gone. I could feel the sweat pouring out of me, coursing down my face, running down my side, soaking through my shirt. It felt horrible but tickled at the same time. If the circumstances were different, I would have wanted to laugh. Instead, I wanted to scream.

"You can take your time," the man said, smiling again. "I'm not in a hurry. Oh, I'm sorry, my name's Nishi, by the way."

The strap finally came loose and I extended the watch to him. "I'm Machida," I told him. I still have no idea why I introduced myself to the man who was robbing me.

"Nice to meet you, Mr. Machida. You said you had a phone too."

'Damn it, why did I say that?' I felt around for the phone in my jacket's inside pocket, but being still threaded through the handle of my briefcase, it was an almost impossible task. All the time, my other hand was frozen around the briefcase handle, unable to let it go.

"Just in case you're wondering," the man, Mr. Nishi, continued, "I don't always do this kind of thing. Actually, I work in a bank."

"Well why don't you just rob the bank?" I blurted out, again demonstrating in the most foolhardy way, the new disconnect between my mouth and my brain. *'Where the hell did that come from? Please don't shoot me!'*

"Good one," Mr. Nishi smiled. "Actually, I've already done that. Just a couple of years ago in fact, and I got away with it. But now I'm a Harvestee, you see, so I'm going to The Terror."

I found the phone and very slowly offered it to Mr. Nishi.

"Thanks very much," Nishi said, suddenly looking a little troubled. "I'm going to The Terror," he said again, as though he was still trying to absorb the awful truth of his situation. He snapped back to the present, to me. "And it's a bit late to turn myself in now: I think my sentence would be a little longer than four days!" He forced a chuckle, but thinking back now, he might have been trying to stop himself from crying. "Plus I don't have the money anymore," he said. "I spent it all. So that's that, as they say. Absolutely nothing I can do about it now. So, I might as well do what I want while I'm still here, eh? And then I thought to myself this morning, 'I've never robbed anyone at gun point before, I wonder how that feels', so here I am, and here we are."

The panicked questions and terrifying conclusions reeled off in my mind as fast as I envisioned the bullets being launched from the gun barrel; *'He's doing this just to know what it feels like? This man's got nothing to lose! Wait a second, if he's really such a lost cause, he can just kill me if wants to. It won't make a single bit of difference to him. Please, please don't kill me!'*

Nishi looked at my phone in his hand and back at me. "Nice phone. I hope you won't mind me using it. Just for fun."

I shook my head enthusiastically. "No, I don't mind at all. You go for it. Please, can I go now? I have to go."

"Yes, of course." Mr. Nishi was acting as though we we're having a perfectly normal conversation. "Have a good day and a Happy Harvest." He bowed again.

I bowed back.

"And feel free to tell anyone you want to that you were mugged. Remember, the name's Nishi."

I wasn't sure it was happening. Was I being let go? I backed away slowly, turned, and started walking. All of the muscles in my back were tensed rigid, trying in some way to prepare for a sudden bang and a pain so intense that I couldn't even imagine it. I didn't want to die. There was so much to do. And I was so close to seeing Naomi again. I told myself that if I kept on walking, I'd be okay. I just needed to turn the corner, it was close, and then I could run, and everything would be okay. But then I heard Nishi's voice again.

"Mr. Machida!"

My mind was screaming, '*Please, let me go. Please don't kill me!*' I didn't want to stop walking, the corner was so very close, but I knew it would be fatally foolish of me to keep going. I stopped and turned around, all very slowly. Nishi was walking toward me, still pointing the gun, still smiling, and there was still no one around.

"I really am sorry about this," he said. "Truly, I was just going to let you go but what with things being as they are, I should be honest with you. After all, there's not much time left and, I have to say, everything I've done, everything I've worked so hard for, it doesn't matter now. None of it matters. It might as well have never mattered; I'm going to The Terror, after all the work I've done for this city." He was struggling to maintain his smile and I could now see the tears welling up in his eyes. "Y'know, I really did just try to accept it," he continued, "Just quietly, y'know, with dignity. I didn't want to cause a fuss. But what's the point in that? How does that help me? I'll let you in on a secret: it doesn't. I'm here suffering and trying not to cause any upset but nobody actually cares. So maybe I should take the opportunity to express myself properly. I mean, it's not like anybody died because of anything I did but I still have to suffer for it because the Harvest is so clever, isn't it. Well, in any case, try not to think of me as a bad man. But I think it's only good balance that if I'm going to The Terror, I should give the Harvest a proper reason to send me there."

Even as the words were still spilling out of Nishi's mouth, I knew the conclusion he was headed for. But rather than a defeated cry, which in all honesty is what I expected, before I could even think, I was swinging my briefcase up at the gun. It all seems like slow-motion now, like I was watching a movie. I certainly don't feel like I was in control of my actions. The two connected, but there was no bang, and suddenly the gun was pointing up in the air. But it was still firmly in Nishi's hand.

'Damn it! In the movies, they always drop the gun!'

Nishi clearly hadn't expected any fight from me. It was like he'd mugged Dr. Jekyll but threatened to kill Mr. Hyde. As he reeled back, I suddenly found I was able to take another swing. This time my case connected firmly with his face and he stumbled back and fell to the ground, gun still in hand. My fingers somehow unlocked and I let go of the briefcase and dove for the gun. All other concerns were secondary. As long as Nishi held onto the weapon, I was as good as dead. My dive was aimed true, and pinning Nishi to the ground with my own body, I grasped the gun with both hands and tried to twist it free but his grip was incredible. The gun wouldn't move. While I struggled with the weapon, he released his other arm from under me and began punching me in the side, though I hardly felt a thing at first. I had to focus on the gun. But I soon began to tire, and as I started to feel the sharp, crippling pain of every punch, I realised Nishi might have been older than me but he had far more stamina than I did; before long, I wouldn't have the strength to wrestle the gun away. As quickly as I could move, I let go of the gun with one hand and I elbowed Nishi in the face. For just a moment, he was weakened, his grip slackened, and I pulled the gun away from him, instinctively twisting it back to face him and pulling the trigger. There was hardly a sound, no loud bang, no shouts from either one of us or screams from sudden passers-by. There was only a muffled *pop* and a burst of red erupted from a small point on Nishi's chest, just to the right of his navy blue tie.

I realise now that even while I was being mugged, the world was still perfect. It only stopped being perfect when Mr. Nishi stopped moving.

6
Trials of A Reluctant Detective.

The Department for Births, Deaths and Marriages is housed in a monolithic sixteen storey building right in the centre of the expansive Civic Plaza. Entry to the Plaza itself means passing through one of five visual security checkpoints. Sometimes these are manned and sometimes they're fronted by the image of what I can only assume is a genuine DBDM worker as I don't think he's handsome enough to be a model. When the man's image greets us, we're surreptitiously checked by a machine. After the visual checkpoint and the four-minute walk through the Plaza's security-sensored grounds, there are three combined public and employee entrances to the DBDM building, all monitored. There are a further nine employee-only guarded entrances at ground level and a total of fifty-two emergency exits situated on various levels, as well as two ground level loading bays for specialist equipment or, on occasion, emergency vehicles. All of these can be used to gain entry if strictly necessary. Another external loading bay is located halfway up the building on the eighth floor and one more is situated on the roof. Each of the fifty-two emergency exits are sensor monitored and set to alarm if opened without inside authorisation, and each loading bay has a manned station and alarm sensors similar to those placed on the emergency exits. As for the three public and employee entrances and the employee-only entrances, each has two security guards, an integrated body scan, Ward Registration Card and Rice Grain scan, and a security pass protocol. Absolutely none of these measures prove to be a problem, and there's no reason why they should. I'm the same man who's turned up for work every weekday and the occasional weekend for five and a half years. However, as I arrive, every procedure seems to take three times longer than normal, like every gesture I make and every sideways glance at a monitor or scanner is being scrutinised by the guards and the machines with extra caution. Surely this isn't really the case. No person knows what I've done; no scanner can read anything on my Rice Grain other than my ID and whatever civic data is held on the central database. Everything should be normal.

It is. Aside from a 'Congratulations, Mr. Machida' postcard propped up against my display screen, a couple of people wishing me good luck, and a slightly tidier desk that I started cleaning yesterday, there's very little here to suggest I'm going away, never to return. This lack of focus on me is a good thing, and I thank my deceased ancestors for looking kindly on me. I'm not a religious man but the tradition my parents and grandparents have taught me about praying to my ancestors every now and again and not angering them seems to be in some way paying off. Sort of. Seeing as I've just accidentally shot and killed someone four days before my Harvest and put myself in an unbelievably horrendous situation, at least one of my ancestors is still very angry with me for something. Maybe one day I'll find out what. But it will be enough if nobody bothers me today; then I'll be in less danger of giving myself away and I can concentrate on what to do. Bizarrely, I wonder for a moment if I should now also add Nishi to the deceased people I occasionally pray to, but I think better of it. Nishi and I aren't related, plus I'm not really sure I believe the thing about praying to the ancestors anyway.

It takes only a moment for my workstation to acknowledge that I'm me before my screen welcomes me to the database and waits expectantly for me to begin doing something. I do nothing.

I sit at my desk for an hour, continuing to do nothing, paralysed by some force I don't understand and made to observe departmental news feeds or fragments of work streams. I can feel each moment vanishing away but I can't do a thing about it. Now there's some kind of stirring in the office, I can tell without looking away from my display, someone is moving between the desks, it's something unscheduled. My department head comes to the centre of the floor and calls for the staff's attention. He has with him another suited man, about mid-thirties, quite athletic-looking.

"Everyone," the department head calls out, "Allow me to introduce to you Mr. Simon Minamoto. He's starting work in the Department for Births, Deaths and Marriages today. Thank you."

Minamoto bows deeply. "I'm Minamoto, it's a pleasure to meet all of you, and I'm very much looking forward to working hard for the department. I also look forward to getting to know you all better." He bows again.

'*That's an interesting touch*,' I find myself thinking. No one ever goes any further than wishing to work hard for the department. It was exactly the same in my case too when I started. '*What an odd thing to say about looking forward to getting to know the staff better*'. But what really strikes me, though I guess it's a trivial thing really, is not what Minamoto has said but that he actually comes across as sincere. He really is looking forward to getting to know the staff better. What a strange man.

"And I have another announcement," my boss continues. "Today we will say goodbye to Nicholas Machida." Immediately I sense all eyes turning to me. It feels horrible. I begin to wonder again whether or not I've missed any blood on my clothing. I checked in the washroom as soon as I arrived but there's still a chance I wasn't thorough enough. Are the other staff members now also wondering why my jacket is still buttoned up? Can they see that I've been crying, that I'm starting to sweat again? I know they expect me to bow so I stand up quickly, bow, and sit down again, almost all before they start to clap. The applause sounds wrong to me. They don't know what they're doing. They're applauding someone who killed a man just this morning. I want to tell them to stop, but I can't say anything, so I try to smile. I can't do this either.

My department head speaks up again. "Perhaps we'll hear something from Mr. Machida this evening. Until then, please have a very good final day with us."

I manage a very quiet, "Thank you", and soon everyone stops clapping and resumes work. No one can tell the ordeal I've just suffered in those few seconds, and it will get worse. My boss hasn't supposed that I might give some kind of farewell speech this evening; he's just told me I will.

I'm only staring at my screen: I'm not thinking; not about work or even about the man I've killed. I wanted to clear my mind in order to think objectively about what I should do, but all I've been able to do is stare. Maybe this means my mind is clear; but now how do I draw it back to a useful thinking state? The words on my screen might have meant something once; important information to be registered here or processed there and so keep the city running smoothly. Now they've mutated into meaningless shapes and blurred lines, black on white, blue on black. They're nothing of consequence: nothing that will help change anything for me or make the slightest bit of difference to the impossible situation I'm in. *None of it matters*. Where have I heard that before?

A red blur appears at the top of my screen and five and a half years of conditioning makes me read it. As the bright red words come into focus, I suddenly fall short of breath and almost throw up. It's a police notice, alerting me that sensitive information is coming through to my workstation and that the transmission is now being routed via the department head. It asks me for my Rice Grain ID number and waits. My hands shake. '*What if this is about that man? What do I do?*' Red-flagged police notices are only ever concerning suspicious deaths. I want to run away from my desk, but I also want to enter my number and avoid arousing suspicion. Either way, I can hardly move. I try breathing deeply again. I've had these police notices come in before, perhaps two or three each year. They're not for regular processing, but rather to fill-in gaps in preliminary police reports. Actual processing of the death and any civil implications for the next of kin are done separately; it's entirely possible this notice has nothing at all to do with anyone called Mr. Nishi. I type my number in slowly, hoping as hard as I can with every key press that the coming information will be something I know nothing about. A flurry of asterisks follows, signifying my department head has entered his own number to confirm his presence, and an empty dialogue box appears. For a couple of seconds, there's nothing, like the computer is mimicking me holding my breath. Someone at the police station now starts typing and the words stream onto my screen:

CASE NUMBER 37828-D: Fatal shooting at 4B-12-10.
RICE GRAIN ID: 18620431. NAME: Nishi, Jon.

*WARD REGISTRATION CARD SCAN: *18620431**
Match
RICE GRAIN REGISTER: 12-08-56428.

I watch the characters flood into the dialogue box and as soon as I read 'fatal shooting', I know my hopes for this to be new information to me are in vain. I feel numb, I need this to stop, but the words keep on coming.

OCCUPATION: Bank Clerk, Royal Bridge Bank.
CAUSE OF DEATH: Single gunshot wound to chest.
**Please add further education, employment, and next of kin details on DBDM form C31 and return to this office.*
**SPECIAL NOTES: Victim was a Harvestee.*
Case being treated as murder.

Murder. The word is like a clanging bell. '*That's not true!*' I cry out in my mind, '*It was an accident!*' I feel suspended in my own body, again unable to move, like the word has some kind of power over me. '*It was an accident.*' I can't even make a sound. I'm frozen. '*I'm not a murderer.*'

There's another flashing red line. The police officer is asking me to confirm receipt of the notice and terminate the link until I'm ready to send back the completed form. After a short time, I don't even remember terminating, only that it's now done and I'm no longer sharing a screen with the police or with my department head, and I feel strangely safer. But now the word '*murder*' comes back to me. '*I can't be a murderer,*' I try to convince myself, '*it was self defence.*'

"Congratulations, Mr. Machida!" I almost jump out of my seat. The smiling Minamoto stands over me and bows. "I'm sorry," he continues, "I didn't mean to startle you. So, you're a Harvestee? You must be pretty excited."

"Yes," I reply. My answer is automatic, the same way I always say, "I'm fine", whenever someone asks me how I am. It's a lie.

"Do you have any special plans before you leave?" Minamoto asks.

I can hardly believe the man is making conversation with me. I want to tell him to go away, that I need time alone to think of a way out of this awful situation, but instead, I utter, "No, no special plans."

"No family here?"

"Parents are in Euchaea. I've got a fiancé there too." My heart wrenches. My parents, Naomi, they're waiting for me in Euchaea but surely I can't go there now. Whatever happens, whether I come up with some kind of solution or not, I won't see my dad, mom, or fiancé again. As much a shock to myself as to Minamoto, I suddenly begin to sob. The new employee leans back a little in surprise and quickly looks around to make sure no one else has seen my little spectacle. Thankfully, the one or two people who've heard my small cry and flinched, pretend not to notice and continue working.

Minamoto hands me a tissue. "I understand," he says, softly. "You've been here your whole life, everything you know is here, and now you have to leave it all behind for good. I guess in some ways it doesn't matter how amazing Euchaea is, it's still hard to leave the place you call home."

I wipe my eyes and try to regain some composure but still I can't muster any words.

"Well, don't be scared of it. One of the great things we're told about Euchaea is that it's all new, but not in an unpleasant way. It's a brand new perfect place in society tailored just for you, and as the Rice Grain knows everything you think and feel, it should be exactly what you need to fit and fulfil you. It's a bit like a fresh start and this old life here with all of its worries are gone; you're free to make the very best of life and really enjoy things." He leans in closer. "Plus you get to fully understand why we have the Harvest, what this city and the filter are all for, since you'll be living in the result of it all. And anyway, once you've spent thirty-four years in Euchaea, that'll feel like home too." Minamoto chuckles slightly. He's trying to cheer me up so I give him an appreciative nod. "I'll let you get on with it," he says, "but seriously, if you don't have anything special planned, let me know. It'd be good to do something together before you leave. Or if you just need to talk or get something off your chest, I'll be around."

Minamoto returns to his new workstation at the far end of the office and I grab another tissue from the desk. I feel embarrassed to have broken down in front of him like that, but really I think my control was extraordinary. In truth, I want to wail out loud with unrelenting tears and beat myself over the head until I lose consciousness. But I can't do that. I don't remember all of Minamoto's speech, but as good as Euchaea might sound, I'm not going there. And even before that terrible Harvest Day, I still have the remainder of this awful life to endure.

Just to add to my misery, I also remember there's a police notice on my computer that takes priority over all of the other work I haven't done today: some faceless officer at the police station is now waiting for some faceless processor at the DBDM to complete a death form and send it back. If I really wanted to, I could solve the case for them right now.

7
The Man Who Was Almost Right.

I duck out to lunch at 12:00 rather than my customary 12:30. I can't bear to be in the office any longer. Compared to the usual level of general politeness at work, people are treating me so very nicely, and it all feels wrong. '*If they only knew what I've done*,' I keep accusing myself. I just can't help it. I have a further reason for taking an early lunch and that is to avoid the possibility of Minamoto collaring me to have lunch with him. There's nothing wrong with Minamoto, and under normal circumstances I might have asked the new employee myself if he'd like to have lunch. I find him interesting, if a little given to speeches. But I need to be alone. It's proven fruitless to try and think through my predicament sitting at my desk, and opening up to Minamoto won't help, nor is it the proper way to deal with it. This is my problem, not anybody else's. I decide on lunch in the park across the road from the Civic Plaza – maybe fresh air will help – and I take a handful of cash from my wallet and leave without saying a word.

I dreaded starting the search through Mr. Nishi's personal details but it all proved painless. Other than a much older sister who'd been called away two Harvests ago, the man had no other immediate relatives, which I almost subconsciously interpreted as 'no one close'. Education and employment details were also fairly standard: nothing about stealing from his employers, though that wasn't at all surprising. His Rice Grain had known all about it but it would only ever surrender those precious hidden memories to the mysterious probing of the Harvest Light. The whole episode of searching through Nishi's past became nothing more than a simple information retrieval exercise, no different than if I'd been asked to do the search on someone I hadn't killed. The form was returned to the police, no suspicion was aroused, and now I'm sitting on a wooden bench under a beautiful blue sky, grass stretching out a hundred metres in front of me, I'm sweltering hot, and my suit jacket is still buttoned up.

I sit for almost the whole of my lunch hour having taken only one bite of my boxed meal. So many things have been going through my mind: trivial and special childhood memories, things I love about my parents and about Naomi, what I'd wanted to say or do when first seeing them upon arriving in Euchaea, how it's taken less than a single morning for my entire life and all I've ever done and dreamed of to be destroyed. Occasionally interrupting my thoughts on what I might possibly do to change what's happened or to convince anyone it was an accident, or how I might somehow escape or delay my Harvest, are cries of delight from children playing, or parents calling after them, or from young couples laughing together on the grass, relaxing. It makes me angry. Other than the last Harvest Week when I lamented so bitterly the impending separation from Naomi, this has always been a good time for me: a few days out of work or school, a time to enjoy being free, a time to be one of *those* relaxing people. Even when my parents were going, I knew I'd see them again so I simply made the most of that week together with them, at home, in the park, or out at some entertainment venue, enjoying the temporary release from responsibility. Now all of these other people are enjoying what I've been robbed of, through no fault of my own, and there's no course for appeal or complaint. It's the ultimate injustice. How can the Rice Grain or the Harvest be considered 'just' and yet things like this happen? If one of these men I see playing baseball with their little kid had found himself confronted by Nishi this morning and killed him… I stop myself. I realise I'm wishing it really had been one of these men playing baseball with their child, rather than me: some inconsequential man I wouldn't miss, some nameless person I wouldn't care about regardless of who killed who. After all, I'm certain none of the men here care that I'm going to go to The Terror. To them, I must look just like an average *salaryman* taking advantage of the weather on his lunch break, not someone who killed a man today and still has the telling splashes of blood on his shirt. Only my Rice Grain really knows what I've done and it's sitting silently on my brainstem, burning me, dragging me toward The Terror with every passing second, and there isn't a thing I can do about it.

I look down at my lunch and I'm almost sick. I start to cry. What difference does any of this make? Whether I eat or not, whether I'm sick or not; it's meaningless. All I've ever done and hoped for has proved meaningless. They carry no weight, no significance, nothing; they simply don't matter. Not to anyone. More meaningless happy shrieks from the children pierce me, and it pulls me down further. There's no point to anything; everything ends in me going to The Terror. None of these things I see around me are any longer of importance, nothing I say or do, nothing anyone else says or does. And I realise something terrible: I've become Mr. Nishi. Now I understand exactly what the man had been suffering, and I stop crying. '*What do you know, maybe he was right. I guess it really would be easy to kill someone*,' my mind wanders. '*After all, it wouldn't make any difference. Not to me, not really. Well, it wouldn't make my suffering or my punishment any worse at least. It's just like Nishi said: he wanted to rob me just for the experience of it, and killing me wouldn't have been any worse in the eyes of the Harvest.*

'*But on the other hand, I guess I wouldn't really want to take someone else's life. It might not mean much to me but it could still have meaning for them, deluded as they are. The world may not be fair, but maybe I still am – at least a little bit. Hey, so maybe I'm not quite the same as Nishi after all. But that still doesn't change anything. I don't want to go to The Terror. I can't go to The Terror.*' The words become faintly audible. "I can't go there. I can't." But my protestations are as useless as they are feeble. There's no one to appeal to, nothing to hope for, only one place I'm headed for, and I simply can't bear it. '*It really would be easy to kill someone,*' I think again. And there I find my solution. I'll kill myself.

8
Departing.

I'm by no means resolved to commit suicide, but it seems like the only solution. Either way, I guess it's some help that it isn't far to walk to the train station, leaving me less time to change my mind about jumping in front of a train. I'm beset by doubts: is this truly the right thing to do, is there no other way? Once I commit to this, there really is no going back – I can't take my own life and then change my mind! I have to be sure there's no other option: but what else is there if I go on living? All I can possibly do is flounder in unbearable fear and depression, waiting to be snatched away to The Terror. It's simply something I can't do. This, however, is something I can.

As soon as I arrive at the station, I realise I should have brought my Ward Registration Card with me to make identifying my body easier. I'm actually quite annoyed with myself that I've forgotten it and the intensity of my annoyance in turn surprises me. I don't usually go anywhere without my Card or my wallet, indeed it's standard practice that everyone carries his or her Ward Registration Card at all times, but my mind was elsewhere when I took an early lunch. No doubt someone in my own department will have to process my death (I wonder who it will be), and I know that if it were me carrying out the task, it would go much more smoothly if the Card and the Rice Grain could be registered together instead of a frustrating couple of hours apart, dragging out a job that should take only half an hour at most. Every processor hates it when that happens. It can bring down his or her personal productivity average, making them look bad, and then it also has a wider effect on the productivity average for the whole department, making us all look bad. My annoyance becomes shame at showing such a lack of consideration for my work colleagues. I had no idea they were so important to me. But I guess there's nothing I can do about it now, and I guess it ultimately doesn't matter.

The next train is due in three minutes. Oddly, I find the idea that I now know exactly when I'm going to die quite elevating. It's almost like having some supernatural insight to know that at 13:14, my life will abruptly end, and hopefully with a minimum of pain.

I sit on the hard plastic platform chair and watch people going to and fro. I wonder why they make the chairs like this? Probably so that people don't get too comfortable and miss their trains – good idea. Maybe that's why I'm the only person sitting down; everyone else is rushing to do something or to get somewhere, I guess they really can't afford to be late. Wherever they're going, whatever they're doing, it must seem important to them and even though I may disagree, even though I now realise that nothing is that important, I have absolutely no desire to deprive them of their sense of purpose. It's something of a comfort – if a somewhat false one – to know that even at this lowest point, I'm still not quite the same as Mr. Nishi: I'm still willing to accept other people's points of view, even if I know they're misguided, and I don't feel I have to kill them for it. This is all my own problem and I'll deal with it.

I can feel the empty seconds of my life ticking away. I should fill them with good thoughts, go out not exactly smiling perhaps, but at least remembering that it hasn't all been a nightmare. I start to think one final time about the good people I've known and cared for, family and friends who've been taken in Harvests ahead of me, those still here in the city, people who might be upset once I'm gone. And I suddenly remember Esther. I have to say goodbye to her! There are other friends who'll stay behind, people who'll miss me, but Esther is different. We've known each other since we were children, since even before I met Naomi. In some ways we're perhaps even as close as Naomi and I; certainly after my fiancé, Esther is without doubt my best, most devoted friend. And she's also a bit of an odd type. I can say this because she knows it's true and because I've said it to her face more times over the years than I can remember. In fact, I'm fairly certain it's become more than an accepted truth and now she thrives on being told; it eggs her on, and I can't honestly say I'm ashamed to be party to this encouraging of her often non-conformist ways in our very conformist society. Her energy, in turn, energises me. Most of the women I know (including Naomi) are quite self-restrained, very lady-like, but Esther has a much more out-going, expressive nature about her (some might call it 'overly expressive'), with perhaps a certain lean toward eccentricity. But both Naomi and I agree that in Esther, these are qualities. She brings an extra dimension of balance to me and my fiancé, a somewhat unchecked emotion to complement my conservative reservation and Naomi's blend of conservative impulsiveness. I'm sure some have missed out on getting to know her true depth and kindness because of perhaps unfortunate first impressions of her not-always-conventional character, but their not getting to know her is ultimately their own loss. Esther is my confidante here, the only person I would even consider telling all to. I know she won't be able to save me from The Terror, but I at least owe her a very grateful 'thank you' for all she's meant to me. I take out my phone and dial quickly.

I don't intend to tell her specifically that I'm going to kill myself; I'm just going to ask how she is and wish her a Happy Harvest, but I'm redirected to her video messaging service. Angry, I almost hang up, but there won't be another chance to say farewell so I force an almost-smile and leave her a message thanking her for everything and telling her that I'll see her around. After I hang up, I say to her, "Sayonara" – *'goodbye'*. And now I have less than one minute to live.

During my silent walk to the station, I considered using the maglev train to end my life as they travel much faster than the regular trains and I'd be almost guaranteed not to feel a thing when it hit me. But there are only five or so maglevs per day so I'd have to wait a couple of hours for the next one, and I believe this is perhaps one of those instances in life that has to be rushed. Also, with a maglev, I'd have to time my leap off the platform precisely. Too late and the air pressure would suck me into the side of the train, causing horrendous and painful injury but not necessarily death; too soon and as the train doesn't actually make contact with the ground, it would simply glide right over me. I would end the day bruised, embarrassed, under arrest, and still alive. With a regular train, there's no such risk. There's more chance that I might feel it, but hopefully the sensation won't last long. I'll find out in a moment.

There's a familiar hard rumble as the train comes round the bend into view. I stand at the near end of the platform so that as I leap out, the driver won't have time to stop and will still be moving fast enough to do the job properly. At around the ten-seconds-to-live mark, I begin to feel nervous, and now scared. But I've already thought this through; there isn't any point in reconsidering. I check one last time that the train is still hurtling along, I take my final deep breath and close my eyes, and I step forward. And my phone rings. The sudden chirpy sound and vibration in my pocket shock me and my steps falter. Should I answer it or ignore it? It could be Esther; but I've already said goodbye; surely nothing anyone wants to call me about now matters? I've thought too long. The blast of warm air from the train passing by forces me to open my eyes and watch my missed chance gradually slow down to ineffectiveness and stop. People get off and get on, and nobody knows how close they came to witnessing something horrific. And nobody cares.

"Can't I even kill myself properly?" I curse as the train pulls away. I don't care if anyone hears me, but I don't think anyone has. Why is everything going wrong? I could have been free from the pull of The Terror now, but instead I'm still standing on the platform, as alive and as condemned as before. My phone is still ringing. There'll be another train in about eight minutes; I decide I can wait that long and return to my hard plastic seat. Taking the phone from my pocket, I'm surprised not to see Esther's name and picture on the display but rather a phone number I don't recognise. Why not answer it? This could be my final conversation.

There's no image, just a faint voice, so I hold the phone to my ear and it switches to 'privacy' mode. The man at the other end of the line doesn't sound familiar. He's in a noisy place and his phone isn't doing a great job of filtering out the background sounds so it's difficult to hear him. "Hello, Mr. Nishi, it's me. Where are you?"

My heart feels like it's stopped. I can't believe this is happening, though I'm not really sure what *this* is. Did the man just ask for Mr. Nishi? But this is my own phone, I'm sure of it: I just called Esther using her name in the phone's memory. I know I didn't pick up Nishi's phone by mistake this morning. I think about hanging up, but the person will only call again. Even if I ignore it, even though I know I'll be dead within the next eight minutes, I still feel terrified, like someone knows what I've done. "Erm, I'm sorry, I'm not Mr. Nishi," I say.

"What? This isn't Harry Nishi?"

I'm suddenly able to breathe again. I remember seeing on the police notice that *my* Mr. Nishi's name was Jon, not Harry. "No, sorry, you've got the wrong number." I'm so relieved that I almost smile.

"Ah, my mistake, very sorry. Please excuse me." The man hangs up and I slump back in my chair, stunned at the traumatic coincidence. *'What are the chances of that? Come on now, Nicholas, keep it together. Not long left.'*

Although the last train departed only a couple of minutes ago, people are already gathering on the platform for the next one so I decide to stand in place, ready. Before I can get up, my phone rings again and I tell myself off for not thinking to switch it off after the previous call. However, just as I'm about to cancel the call, I see Esther's name and picture on the display. The same questions run through my mind again as when I stood at the edge of the platform with the train approaching: should I answer it? What more is there to say? But stronger than any questions I have comes the desire to see a friendly face and hear a friendly voice one last time. I answer.

The picture of Esther on my phone screen suddenly bursts into life, her short hair flapping across her thin, pale face as she yells out, "Hi, Nick!" It feels like so long since I last heard a sound so pleasant. I may have even forgotten that nice feelings exist. "I just got your message," she continues. "What was all that about? Did you have a sentimentality fit or something?"

It's typical Esther and I want to smile but I can't. "No, nothing like that."

"Well, don't worry," she says, "I haven't changed my mind. I'll be back well before your Harvest to see you off."

"Yes, I know. I just wanted to call."

"Oh, Nick," she sighs, like a doting parent, her face now filling the whole display, "You're like my cat – if I ever get a cat. You're so 'clingy'. In a nice way. I want my cat to be clingy."

"Esther, what are you talking about?" Now I'm nearly in danger of smiling.

"Oh, ignore me. So, what's the matter, you Euchaean citizen, you? You're looking quite down."

Something is happening. I'm starting to miss Esther. I don't want to kill myself without saying a proper goodbye to her, without seeing her in person or at least being honest about what I'm going to do. It's not right. It's not fair on her. But if I see her, surely that will make things more difficult for both of us? Surely *that* won't be fair on her? Better to get this suicide over with. Just do it, and there'll be nothing more to think about. But why deprive myself of one last happy sensation, pointless as it may be? What real difference will it make to me not to see her? The end result will still be the same, only that if I wait, I'll at least have had the pleasure of being with my friend again and even being able to explain my actions. But I can't wait, the prospect of The Terror is torturing me, and I can't possibly tell her over the phone what I'm about to do. "Esther, something terrible's happened." The words slip out before I even realise I'm speaking. "I need to see you."

"Nicholas, what is it? What's the matter?" There's suddenly not so much of a smile on Esther's face now.

I wish I hadn't said anything. I want to explain everything to her now but not here, not with people all around. I put the phone to my ear, switching it to private mode again, but even this doesn't feel secure.

"Nicholas, what are you doing? Where's your picture? Are you still there?"

"I – I can't say what the problem is right now. What time will you be back?"

"I can't get back until tomorrow. Nicholas, what's wrong?"

Tomorrow? It might as well be in four days. The announcement for the next train sounds.

"Nicholas, where are you?" There's a growing anxiousness in Esther's voice. "Go home! Wherever you are now, just go home and stay there. I'll get away first thing in the morning and be back there before lunchtime, I promise. Can you hear me?"

It's a struggle to say "yes".

"Promise me you'll go home right now and wait for me."

I want to tell her to calm down but no words come out. Surely I haven't let slip anything about my intentions, and she can't have guessed what I'm going to do? But Esther has always been intuitive; maybe she heard the station announcement and the tremble in my voice, and now she's conjured up an image of some 'terrible' thing I can't tell her about. It isn't unheard of for depressed Harvestees to throw themselves under trains and perhaps this is the unfounded conclusion her overactive imagination has jumped to. Of course, she's absolutely correct, but there's no way for her to know this. I've never been the suicidal type. But today has been an exceptional day: these aren't thoughts I'd usually entertain.

"Okay, I'm going home," I eventually say. But I'm not sure if I will. And I add, "I'll wait for you." But I'm not sure if I'll do that either.

Esther sounds like her voice is cracking. "Nicholas, I'll be back soon, I promise. Just wait for me."

"Sure," I say, and I wait until Esther hangs up. *'I really don't know if this is such a good idea,'* I think, but I'm already leaving the station.

9
Travelling Fellows.

I don't bother returning to work. I know some kind of 'leaving presentation' is supposed to take place in my honour, and although it truly does ache that I'm neglecting my responsibility to give a proper farewell speech to my work colleagues, the fact that I intended to be dead by this time anyway gives me some relief. I sit in the public coffee shop of another large company building, staring at my remaining half cup of coffee instead of tying up loose ends at my own place of work or clearing my desk: this is merely a stay of execution. I'm still as good as dead.

Rather than heading straight for the monorail home after leaving the train station, I wandered around the city, for how long I'm not sure, perhaps a couple of hours, not really taking in my surroundings like I did first thing this morning. This morning seems like so long ago: I was a different man back then! Instead, I've been in a daze, numb partially because of one fate that might await me: my being spirited away to The Terror by the great Harvest Light in four days, and the other, more probable fate: my fast approaching death. It's a choice I could never have imagined, a situation I wouldn't wish on anyone, not even Mr. Nishi, but it's all mine alone. Still, even in my hopeless state, I no longer allow myself to question my decision to wait for Esther: a kind word from a good friend is all I have to look forward to, and perhaps it's all I need to finally send me on my way.

The man at the table next to me stands and loses grip of his saucer, dropping his cup and splashing dregs of coffee over his table. I try to ignore him, but he asks me if he can use the paper napkins that are sitting in the holder in front of me. I nod slightly and he reaches over and takes them.

"Thanks," he says. "Sorry about that. I'm quite nervous. I'm up for Harvest in four days."

I stop ignoring him. "Really?" I immediately wish I hadn't said anything. The last thing I want is a conversation with another Harvestee, particularly one who in all likelihood is going to Euchaea.

"Yes," the man says. "I was certainly surprised when I found out I was a Harvestee this time. I've been here fifty-three years. I kind of believed it'd never happen; I mean you get used to a place after so long. Still, I guess once I've spent fifty-three years in Euchaea, that'll feel like home too."

I've heard something like that just recently. I rack my brain: it was Minamoto. *"Once you've spent thirty-four years in Euchaea, that'll feel like home too"*. They're both right, I suppose. *'Hang on. How the hell did Minamoto know I'm thirty-four?'*

"Not that there's any guarantee I'm going to Euchaea," the man continues. "But Euchaea, The Terror, what does it matter? I mean, who even knows if there's any difference? Either one of them, they're not this place. This place is home."

I'm not certain I'm hearing or at least understanding this man correctly: surely he isn't indifferent about the possibility of going to The Terror? Suddenly I find myself saying to him, "Are you serious?"

"Of course I'm serious." The man looks at me as though he really doesn't understand why I'd question him.

"You honestly don't mind whether you go to Euchaea or The Terror?" I ask.

"Of course I mind. Who wouldn't? I want to go to Euchaea just like everyone else, but what I'm saying is this: 'The Scrutiny of Harold Kanagawa', all of the first Harvests, they were so very long ago. Who's to say things haven't changed a lot in The Terror, or even in Euchaea? The fact of the matter is that I'm leaving this place and I'd rather not. Still, that being the case, I've hedged my bets for Euchaea. Better safe than sorry. Not that you can really be *sure* you're safe." He indicates the spilled coffee. "I'm still nervous."

I'm not sure why I question him further. Perhaps it's because I've never heard this take on the Harvest before. Perhaps I'm not so resolved to kill myself after all and I'm still looking for some other way out. "What do you mean, 'hedged your bets'?"

"What?" the man looks confused again and sits back down. "I don't mean to be rude, but are you from here? *Hedged my bets*," he says again. "Y'know, obey the law, do the honourable thing, keep tradition, don't rock the boat. I've just done what's been expected of me. You can't go wrong with that."

'Well that's what I've done,' I agree, but really I'm acknowledging the injustice of it all.

"And I haven't stolen money or killed anyone," the man innocently adds.

'Damn!'

"Sounds like the odds are in my favour," he continues. "That doesn't stop me thinking about delaying though. As I said, this is home."

'Delaying!' I nearly knock my own cup off the table. "Delaying?" Is there another way I haven't considered? "Is delaying possible?" I'm trying not to sound too curious or hopeful.

"Wow, maybe you shouldn't drink so much coffee," the man chuckles as I steady my cup. "Are you up for Harvest too?"

"I'm just interested."

"Well, some people say you can delay your Harvest by drinking water that's had some special type of electric current passed through it."

"What?"

"It allegedly has some sort of effect on your Rice Grain or your nanobots or something. I'm not entirely sure what, I don't think it's ever been proven, but they say it's supposed to make your Grain hard to read, and the more you drink over time, the more affected your Grain becomes until you skip a Harvest or two. Sounds good, doesn't it?"

I think the idea actually sounds quite foolish, but if there's even a slight chance of delaying my Harvest, I'll take it. But why am I only hearing about this now? Is this man trying to sell me something? I really don't want to spend my final days being mugged and conned. I say, "So if you don't want to leave, why haven't you done this?"

"I have," he replies. "I'm hedging my bets, remember? Anything and everything. Well, almost."

I have to ask. "Where can I get some of it?"

"People your age really don't pay attention, do you? What do you mean, where can you get some of it? What do you think that water is that you and everyone else sips every New Year and every Half Year?"

He's right, and I can hardly believe I've never thought about it before. Every New Year and every beginning of the sixth month, it's traditional to buy special bottles of a slightly metallic-tasting water, or to go to a temple to exchange trinkets for little cups of it, and we all drink it down. It's just part of the routine, something we've always done, something everyone has always done, so I've never thought to ask why we do it. I can't believe this has been for the purpose of delaying Harvest all along. "But why would everyone want to delay their Harvest? Doesn't everyone want to go to

Euchaea?" I'm suddenly beginning to feel like I really don't understand the world anymore.

The man sighs like I'm some kind of disappointing student. "You really don't pay attention. It's just tradition. Of course everyone wants to go to Euchaea. This water thing was probably started a long time ago by some important person who didn't want to be taken away from here, and now it's just part of the norm. But everybody knows – or everybody's supposed to know – drinking the water twice a year won't do anything. They say you have to take little sips every day for decades if it's to get into your system and have any effect. I've been drinking it every day since my late teens."

"You're kidding me." I'm quite stunned at what I'm learning and at this man's apparent efforts to delay his Harvest, but perhaps more than that, I'm tremendously disappointed to know that I've missed this possible opportunity.

"No, I'm not kidding. Every morning, first thing. I don't actually believe a word of it, though. Never have, but what does it matter? I drink the water and that base is covered. End of story."

"You don't believe it? But you said you'd been here fifty-three years. You said you thought your Harvest would never happen. Surely that means it must have worked a little?"

"Maybe, maybe not." The man honestly doesn't appear to care. "Maybe there is an element of truth to it, but I don't think so. Anyway, there are people older than me here who haven't been drinking the water every day. You just never know."

The possibility of postponement, in any form, unexpectedly begins to drip a curious sense of purpose back into my life. It's nothing concrete, nothing to say there's any real way at all of delaying my Harvest, but suddenly the thought of killing myself seems somewhat premature. I remind myself that the decision to commit suicide is the last decision I'll ever make, so I really should be sure to weigh all of the possibilities properly. This time, not trying so hard to hide my real interest, I ask, "Do you know of any other ways to delay your Harvest?"

"Are you thinking of trying something?" the man smiles. "Not so eager to leave either? Well, there are almost certainly other ways. It can't be impossible. Tell you what, give me a call sometime. I have to go now, but it'd be good to chat." He stands up and hands me his business card. "But within four days, remember! I won't be here after that."

"Sure thing," I say to him, actually believing I might even call him.

As the man leaves the coffee shop, I immediately begin to wonder if this too is the right thing to do. I can already feel my resolve for killing myself waning. Surely over time, it will only decrease more, making the job harder. Perhaps I should go back to the station and do it now, but no, I want to see Esther first at least. I've already decided that. And maybe, if I feel like it, I might even fit in a drink with that man too, just to see if he has any ideas. So many choices: none of them particularly good ones. I look at the business card he's just given me. His name's Tristan Kato, and I simultaneously grin and frown. "Just as I thought," I say quietly, reading on. "A salesman."

10
An Entirely Unexpected Find In The Dark.

It's a strange thing, standing on the monorail platform again. I can't help thinking back to the train station, watching the 13:14 train approach, edging myself toward it. Over and over in my mind, I complete the task, leaping off the platform and putting an end to my troubles, and over and over, I wonder if I've done the right thing by delaying. Naomi really wouldn't be proud of this lingering indecision! When the monorail finally comes, I even imagine stepping out into its path, but I know I won't do it. The monorail is too slow, it would hurt incredibly, and there's a chance I might not even die. And besides, there are reasons why I've delayed, things I need to do, like see Esther, and maybe Mr. Kato the salesman too.

It's already dark by the time I get back to my own station. As I walk home, I try massaging the base of my skull again, but it doesn't help. Not even a little. I'm tense beyond anything I've experienced before and nothing short of being completely exonerated for Nishi's death, or dead myself, is going to alleviate this stress. *'And which of those is more likely?'* I turn the corner toward my apartment building and I almost let out a gasp. A police car is parked right in front of my ground floor apartment. I freeze. An officer who's obviously been there a while is pacing back and forth in front of my door, occasionally stopping to look through the letterbox and calling out, "Mr. Machida! Are you there? Can you hear me?" Another officer soon appears from the rear of the apartment and says something to the first, shaking his head.

'They've come for me! They've discovered who killed Nishi!' I slowly step back around the corner, hoping with all hope that the officers don't see me. Thankfully, they don't seem to have noticed and as soon as I'm out of sight, I turn and hurry back toward the monorail station. I don't know where I'm going to go but I can't go back home. *'But how could they know it was me? I cleaned the gun, I didn't leave any of my things behind.'* I look down at my jacket, still fastened. None of my own blood was shed at the scene either. I'm no crime expert but I've read novels and watched movies: can they have traced me by my sweat? It might be possible, but it's unlikely. *'So how the hell did they know it was me?'* I can feel tears beginning to well up again. In a single day, I've killed a man, failed to commit suicide, and now I'm attempting to escape from the law. This already unimaginable nightmare has just got worse.

It doesn't take long for the monorail to arrive and I sit onboard, going where, I don't know. It feels like I've just run a marathon to get here; I'm exhausted and my heart is pounding, my hands involuntarily begin to shake and the whole carriage is suddenly spinning. At first I think we're about to crash, but none of the other passengers are reacting. It's just me. It feels like my nose is running now but it isn't, it's bleeding. A kind passenger hands me a tissue after watching me fruitlessly search my pockets for something to absorb the blood and I rest my head back against the window until the spinning stops. *'How has all of this happened?'* I ask myself repeatedly. I'm just a civil servant; I've never really hurt anyone, not until this morning. What have I done to deserve this?

After a few minutes, the blood stops dripping and I push the tissue straight into my pocket so as not to look at the bright red: I can't bear to see more blood. I need to think; I need to get away, but where to? I have an idea: Esther's place. For now, I'll stay there. I can't sleep outside her front door until she returns tomorrow, but I can go to a hotel near her station. And I'll pay cash like I did for this monorail journey, just in case the police try to track me down by my Rice Grain transactions. Not thinking clearly, I paid for my drink at the coffee shop and the monorail home by having my Rice Grain scanned and charged directly to my account like I usually do. I'm almost certain this means they now know where I was an hour ago and what time I set off for home. I can't let them get any closer. I still have enough cash in my pocket to pay for a night in a very cheap hotel so I can survive for the time being; I'll just have to try and remember to do everything anonymously from now on.

I'm suddenly aware how much I'm starting to sound and feel like a fugitive: I feel safer knowing that phone conversations aren't monitored, it's some comfort to me that it's possible to get by on cash for while, I'm greatly relieved at the fact that there's no satellite system for tracking people's Rice Grain movements. Having such a tracking system always made sense to me – it still does – so I've often wondered why there are always objections whenever it's proposed. Citing an invasion of privacy or a loss of the right to anonymity, as a lot of people seem to, has never really convinced me. Yes, maybe some civil liberties will be lost but these are minimal and perhaps not even noticeable to the law-abiding. If it means having a system where criminals can be tracked or missing persons found, isn't that a good thing? And surely a measure of personal anonymity can still be maintained somehow. Isn't that why we have the option to use cash – *the anonymous currency* – for so many things instead of being forced to make every transaction using our Rice Grain? It's precisely so that we're not tracked the whole time. This curious resistance to a tracking system is very out of step, I feel, with the over all sense of obedience and 'everything for the greater good' we have in the city. I hope I don't sound too much like a paranoid conspiracy theorist when I say I suspect perhaps powerful and corrupt citizens are behind the swaying of the vote against it. But right now, I'm very glad things are the way they are. If the tracking system existed, the police would instantly have been able to place me at the scene of Nishi's death at the exact moment he was shot, and they would have found and arrested me before lunchtime. There really would be no escape. Maybe I sound like a hypocrite, but if I could express my appreciation to one of those powerful and corrupt citizens right now, I would.

One monorail change at the next hub four more stops along puts me on the line into Esther's ward and I can soon see the familiar neon gambling parlour signs where I usually get off and walk. The signs are telling people that today may be their lucky day. I know it isn't mine. I check into a small hotel near Esther's apartment under the name Nishi (I haven't prepared beforehand not to give my own name and Nishi is the first one that springs to mind when the receptionist asks me). Now I'm lying in a capsule room, two metres long, one metre wide, and one and a quarter metres deep, and I'm feeling sick that the people downstairs think my name's Nishi. I've taken the man's life and now I've also taken his identity. But that too was an accident, a reflex action, completely involuntary. Not that any of that will matter to the police.

It's hard to sleep and I spend at least a couple of hours staring at the ceiling or at the wall. My mind is racing, but for a while it's difficult to grasp hold of any thoughts in particular. I can only see vague shapes of problems: a dead body or a policeman, some kind of torture or torment, a variety of suicide options, but they all blur from one horrible form to the next, preventing me from concentrating on any one thing. Being enclosed in this capsule also doesn't help; I feel as though I'm lying in my own tomb. '*Maybe that's not such a bad thing*,' I think. '*Surely I'm better off dead than in The Terror.*' I don't know what happens to people when they die: maybe something, maybe nothing. There are lots of different theories. If I were a gambling man, I'd 'hedge my bets' like Tristan Kato, the salesman, and gamble on there being 'something': Heaven and Hell, something like that. At least if I'm right, I can try and do something about going to Heaven before it's too late and I die, and if I'm wrong and there's nothing, I won't care because I'll be dead. But all I'm familiar with at this moment is this life, and it's all gone wrong. I think again about turning myself in and throwing myself on the mercy of the police. I think about the advantages and the disadvantages of killing myself now or waiting to see Esther. I compare Kato the salesman's and Minamoto, my work colleague's contrasting takes on the Harvest, and my own disastrous circumstances. There are no solutions in any of my thoughts: only dead-ends and regrets.

Finally, my mind returns to the police, and I'm startled by a possibility I haven't previously considered. Outside my apartment, there had only been two police officers. If they'd come to arrest me for murder, surely there would have been more of them? I assume so, at least. But why else would the police come to my apartment? Esther? She'd never have called them. And suddenly I realise: someone at work must have told them I hadn't returned this afternoon. Many people at the office know I'm a Harvestee and a few noticed me crying this morning. Probably some concerned soul at the DBDM – or perhaps just a colleague wishing to avoid having to register yet another Harvest suicide – must have alerted the police. That has to be the answer. The police can't possibly know that I killed Mr. Nishi; they must have been at my apartment just to check I hadn't committed suicide as I didn't return to work! Seeing as they didn't find me, it stands to reason that they'll be looking for me (but only once I've been missing for twenty-four hours), which although being sought by the police as a missing person isn't good, it's not anywhere near as bad as being hunted for murder. I'm silently impressed with myself for looking on the bright side.

I wonder which kind soul at the office called the police? Could it have been Minamoto? No, he's new to the department, it's not his place to do so. If anyone, it must have been my department head, probably alerted to my absence by some work colleague whom I'll never be able to acknowledge personally.

I've in no way expected to feel anything other than fear and depression tonight, but as I lay here theorising, I experience a strange comfort in the knowledge that the people in the office might actually care about me in some way.

11

The Sayonara Detour (And The Possibility of Cake).

I can hear a soft oscillating tone coming from somewhere close by. Rather than shocking me out of my sleep, it seems to be gradually drawing me toward a waking state and the feeling is rather soothing. If it's an alarm, I wish I owned one like it. It would have been much nicer to wake each morning being gently coerced out of slumber instead of having my own comparatively harsh 'bubble sound' alarm interrupting every night's sleep and shoving me out to work. Still, I don't suppose any of that matters now – I'm probably never going to hear it again. I turn over to where the sound seems to be coming from and a small panel beside my head flashes into life. The polite face of the receptionist downstairs bulges out of the screen toward me and says, "Sorry to wake you, Mr. Nishi, but your car has arrived. The driver is waiting for you in reception. Please come down to collect your things." The image disappears before I have time to tell her I haven't ordered a car. I'm scared. Who has sent someone to pick me up? It won't be work, they don't know where I am, and as far as I'm aware, the police aren't in the habit of sending mysterious drivers to arrest people. Once again, I don't think this has anything to do with Esther either. What should I do? Should I run? Should I call back and tell the receptionist there's been a mistake. Surely this is just a misunderstanding and the driver is for one of the other guests. But while I've been thinking, I've crawled out of the capsule and made my way downstairs to reception. I hate it when that happens. I get so caught up in my thoughts that my body switches to autopilot and only informs me of what it's doing once it's done it. I don't even remember getting dressed, but here I am, back in my grey suit. It's quite disorientating.

I'm standing in the lobby now and I still feel like I should run, but there are clusters of people gathered in front of every exit. If I didn't know better, I'd think they were deliberately standing there to stop me leaving. I see the receptionist very politely beckoning me over to the desk so I go to her and she hands me a brown storage cylinder. It has a misted outer casing to stop people seeing inside, and my name, 'JON NISHI', is printed in large blue letters along the side of it. "Here are your belongings, Mr. Nishi," she says. "Please check to make sure everything is here."

I pull the top off the cylinder and look inside but it's empty. "There's nothing in here," I tell her.

The receptionist laughs as though I made a joke, but when she sees I'm serious, she takes the cylinder back and looks inside. She looks up at me again and tips the contents of the cylinder out onto the desk. There was nothing in there when I looked, I'm sure of it. On the desk is my wallet, my apartment key with a real human eyeball and thumb attached to it by a small chain, a rice ball snack wrapped in crispy seaweed, and an antique pistol.

"Are these items yours?" the receptionist asks.

"Yes, I think so," I say. They seem familiar, even the pistol. I don't know why. Maybe I should've said they were all mine except for that.

The woman slides everything back into the cylinder and hands it back to me. "Here's your driver," she says, indicating behind me, and I turn around. A chauffeur, complete with cap, gloves, and winged trousers, bows and asks me to follow him out to the car. I comply, though I don't know why I'm following him; maybe it's because I'm confused. Surely it would be better to run. I consider making my escape once we're past one of the groups of people standing by the exit but as soon as we pass them and step outside, I see that I'm wearing binders on my wrists and ankles. There's just enough freedom of movement to shuffle my legs as fast as the chauffeur is walking.

The car he leads me to is large and black, and it has a sleekness to it that is more elegant than sporty, like its design has been based on a predecessor that might have been used for transporting royalty. I'm immediately drawn to its look but somehow it doesn't appear 'right'. At first, I can't think what's so odd about what I'm seeing, but now I realise that the light is being completely absorbed by the car's black finish. I can see no reflections from it at all, not sunlight, not even the chauffeur or myself as we approach. The chauffeur opens the back door, helps me inside, closes the door again, and as soon as he does so, the binders vanish. This is all a little bit odd so why is none of it shocking me? And why does the car look so much smaller on the inside? The driver's seat is so close to me, there's hardly enough room for me to sit straight, and when the chauffeur climbs inside, the back of his seat pushes up against my knees. He activates a screen on the back of the seat right in front of me. "Good morning, Mr. Nishi," he says. His voice sounds muffled and distorted coming from the screen, and I wonder why he's bothering as I can hear him perfectly well without it. "Where would you like to go?"

"Where would I like to go?" I think this is the first time I've been properly confused today, despite the slightly bizarre way the morning has unfolded so far. "I don't understand? I didn't order a car. I don't want to go anywhere."

"You have to go somewhere," the chauffeur says. "You can't stay here forever." I see his eyes narrow in the screen. "And don't try to be clever and say you'd like to go nowhere. I've had that from passengers before. Nowhere isn't the absence of somewhere. When you're nowhere, you're there, so you're somewhere."

I'm trying to follow. "Well, if nowhere is somewhere, can't I go nowhere?"

"You *are* nowhere. This city is the equivalent of nowhere." He raises his eyebrows. "Not quite what you thought nowhere would be, is it?"

I have to admit he's right. I always thought of nowhere – on the odd occasion that I actually did think about being or going nowhere – as being away from everyone and everything I know: as taking a break from my life in the city. How was I supposed to have known that being here with everyone and everything I know has been 'nowhere' all along?

"Don't be disheartened, Mr. Nishi," the chauffeur says. I think he can tell I'm starting to feel lost. "The word 'nowhere' is just a concept, of sorts. Everybody here is nowhere. But everybody still goes somewhere."

I think I understand – maybe. I decide to try my luck. "Okay then. I'd like to go to Euchaea please." Surely it can't hurt to ask.

The chauffeur chuckles and I'm immediately disappointed. "That's very funny, Mr. Nishi, but you know you can't go there. You've been stealing from the bank and I'm afraid we can't have that."

I suddenly feel angry with him. "How was I supposed to know this would happen?" I protest. "It wasn't like anybody died!"

"Far be it from me to argue," the chauffeur says, "but you haven't been living in isolation, Mr. Nishi. Everybody in the city knows how to live; everybody knows not to break the law. You can't say you weren't told. I'm sorry."

Just as suddenly as I became angry, my anger turns into distress. "Are you taking me to The Terror? Please don't do it! You asked me where I want to go! Why did you ask if you're going to take me there anyway? I don't want to go to The Terror!" I reach for the door handle but it disappears before I can grab it.

"I asked because I'm not taking you there quite yet. Everybody going to The Terror is given a little detour like this. Think of it as a last request on your way to where you're going to spend the rest of your days: a 'Sayonara Tour', if you like. You get to go wherever you want or do whatever you want, sort of, and then I come back for you. And I will come back for you – there's no getting away from what you've done."

Although I already know there's no escaping my crime, hearing those words from another person, *'there's no getting away from what you've done'*, it makes my situation feel even more painful and even more hopeless. I'm so distressed I almost want to be sick, and it doesn't help my stomach when the chauffeur suddenly launches the car up into the nearest sky lane, even though I haven't told him where to go yet.

"Try not to worry so much, Mr. Nishi," the chauffeur says, turning in his seat to face me. Strangely, it seems like it's the first time I'm seeing his face. He looks quite different than he does on the screen and has a large bushy beard that I hadn't noticed before; it's certainly not the type I'd grow if I were going to be a chauffeur. "The city is your oyster. What would you really like to do? Come on, be creative."

"Shouldn't you be looking where you're going?" I ask him.

"What would be the point in that?" he says. "You haven't told me where we're going yet."

We start to veer out of our lane toward oncoming traffic but the autopilot doesn't sound an alert or correct our path. "What are you doing?" I shout at him, grabbing the edge of my seat.

"Going nowhere, it seems," the chauffeur frowns.

"Okay, just face the front and I'll think of something!" I cry out as we bounce off the side of a smaller car, missing a head-on collision by sheer miracle.

The chauffeur, apparently unflustered by the scrape, turns to the front again and retakes control of the vehicle. "So, what'll it be? You're my fourth passenger today so you've got competition to make it a good choice."

My heart is racing after our near miss; how is the chauffeur so calm? I eventually ask him, "What did the other three passengers pick?"

"The first booked himself into the Tower Diamond Hotel, the most expensive in the city if I'm not mistaken. He's living it up. I think he also had some women brought in. Y'know what I mean?"

I'm not feeling inspired.

"The second one couldn't handle it. Took the pistol and blew her own brains out in the back of my car."

"What? Here?" Now I really do feel sick.

"Yes, there. But don't worry. It's all clean now. And she's safely tucked away in the boot. She won't bother you."

"She's in the boot?" I spring forward from my seat, not that there's really any room to do so.

"Well I wasn't going to leave her sitting beside you. This isn't a bus. And the third one just wanted to stay with her family so I took her on a quick tour of places she hadn't been to before and then dropped her home again. Actually, that one was quite boring. I'll pick them all up again later – well, two of them. Mr. Nishi, what are you doing?"

I'm horrified to see that while the man has been talking, I've dipped my hand into the storage cylinder and taken out the pistol and now I'm pointing it at the back of his head.

"I don't know what I'm doing," I tell him quite honestly, "but I don't want you to take me to The Terror! Please can't you just leave me alone?"

The chauffeur doesn't seem at all concerned that I might kill him. "We have this system for a reason, Mr. Nishi. Although some exceptions to some rules are sometimes made, everybody knows what and what not to do."

"You've already said that!" I want to shoot him. It's the only way to stop him from taking me away.

"If you shoot me, we'll crash and you'll die. Why don't you just shoot yourself instead? There's still plenty of room in the boot."

I can't believe how calm he is. "You're not in any position to try and be smart with me," I say. I think my confusion may be showing through because I'm not speaking as angrily as I intend to.

The chauffeur looks out of the side window toward the ground. "It's a very long way down, Mr. Nishi. You're the one who's not in any position to try and be smart – or stupid, or whatever it is you're doing. Maybe you should clear your head a little."

We've suddenly landed in a quiet street. I don't remember the descent at all, but we're parked and the door beside me is open. The chauffeur turns to face me again so the barrel of the pistol is now touching the tip of his nose.

"Out you get, Mr. Nishi. Take a walk, go crazy, let your hair down. Just do something. But don't take too long about it because I'll be back for you shortly." Before I can say or do anything to respond, I'm suddenly standing on the pavement, pistol still in hand, watching the externally large black car fly away, and thinking to myself how unsympathetic some chauffeurs are.

Angrily, I fire off a couple of shots in the general direction of the disappearing vehicle and set off down the small street closest to me. There's no point just standing here, waiting for him to come back and get me: I might as well do something. Maybe I could try hiding. No, I already know he'll find me. This is all so unfair. Why am I being made to suffer just because of a crime I committed years ago? I don't even remember now how much money it was that I stole. Why should something so relatively trivial have such a damning effect on the rest of my life? If I'd known – or properly understood – that this would happen, I'd have made the most of my life here. I wouldn't have bothered going through the motions of keeping the law and maintaining harmony. What's it all for now? What good has it done me? I could have done more than steal from the bank. I could have done so many things! I would have robbed people. I could rob this poor sap heading toward me now. The unlucky man is probably just out for a walk, like me, but I bet he didn't think to carry a pistol with him this morning. Score one for me! I'll do it!

I should have robbed lots of people and become famous: Nishi, the most notorious mugger in the entire megatropolis. That would be nice. That would be a proper reason to go to The Terror. Or murder! No, *that* would be a proper reason. I don't think I'd murder lots of people – just one or two. And maybe only bad people. I imagine doing something like that might set me up nicely for a life in The Terror: who knows how many people I might have to kill there? Maybe it'll be better for me to start getting used to killing people now, and why not kill two birds with one stone, as it were, and really justify my going there at the same time. What did the chauffeur say? *'Go crazy, let my hair down'*. I might as well. And it's not as though I'm going to kill this man I've just robbed for absolutely no reason at all. He's dying because I need to prepare myself. He's dying because I need practice.

I feel a little disappointed that I don't remember actually pulling the trigger and killing the man. After all, part of the reason for killing him in the first place was so that I know what it feels like to kill someone, so I can be better prepared for such eventualities in The Terror. But the deed is done and the man is dead. There's a little spot of red forming in the centre of his chest and it makes a huge contrast to his gleaming white office shirt. I feel a little sorry for him. I can still feel the tension in my hand from having gripped the pistol tighter to pull the trigger but my heart isn't beating quickly; I can't feel the adrenaline coursing through me, invigorating my senses. I don't feel anything for myself. All I know is that I've done what I wanted to do and nothing has changed, and now all I have left is to wait for the chauffeur. Perhaps when he lands, I can shoot him too. Maybe even steal his car.

"Oh, I wouldn't bother trying to shoot me," I hear the chauffeur's voice behind me. He's parked only a few metres away with his window open. "You're out of bullets."

I know he's right without even looking.

"Do you feel better now?" he asks.

"No," I answer. "Can't you come back later? I thought you were going to pick up the others first."

"I never said that. And besides, they're still busy. You're done."

"I'm not done! I want a few more days! Can't you just give me that?"

The back door of the car swings open. "You're just postponing the inevitable. You know where you're going, and sitting around hoping it'll all go away isn't going to help you. Get in the car."

I'm about to refuse, but I'm already sitting in the back, squashed up against the driver's seat, and the door slams shut again. The car takes off and the chauffeur activates his screen.

"You shouldn't be here, y'know," he says.

"I know!" I cry. "I don't want to be here!"

"No, I mean this isn't you: all this wanting to rob and kill. Why are you doing it?"

I honestly don't know why. I know I don't feel like myself, but I can't seem to remember who *I* am supposed to be, and I can't break out of this robbing and killing mindset. "Can't you help me please?" I ask, pitifully.

"Not really. But I'd stop worrying if I were you, this is probably only a dream anyway."

As soon as the chauffeur says this, I get an odd feeling in my stomach. It's not the sick feeling; it's more like anxious, hopeful butterflies. Although nothing seems particularly unusual, except perhaps for the dead woman sitting beside me whom I hadn't noticed earlier, I'm beginning to believe I'm not actually here in the car. This is very strange, almost like I'm no longer in control of my own thoughts, but it's also very liberating. And it's not just wishful thinking: I try to think back through everything that's happened since being picked up at the hotel, and the more I think about everything, the less it seems to have any coherence or make any sense. It's quite disorientating. The chauffeur may be right. "You think this is a dream? Does this mean that none of this is happening?" I ask, unable to disguise the hope in my voice.

"I'd guess so. None of this stuff going on now is happening," the chauffeur says, "but I think you still killed someone."

"Yeah, I forgot about that."

"So have you decided where you want to go now?"

I'm a little confused again. "I thought I didn't have a choice now. I thought you were going to take me to The Terror?"

"I was, but that was before we realised you're probably dreaming. So I guess you can go anywhere you like now. Except Euchaea."

"Alright then," I say, somewhat relieved – disappointed that I can't go to Euchaea, but relieved I'm not being taken to The Terror. "Anywhere I like? I'd like to go back to sleep please."

"Good choice," says the chauffeur. "Probably the best yet."

I dream that I'm rowing a boat on a still lake and there's an eagle and a fish in the boat with me. Both of them are eating my sandwiches while I row, but I don't mind because the eagle is going to go hunting for cakes afterward. I ask the eagle if this is supposed to mean anything and he says, "No". It's a nice dream.

12
The Suicide Doctor.

I'm woken by my ringing phone. The transition from eating cakes in the open air beside a beautiful lake and not having a care in the world, to suddenly being laid low in an inexpensive composite plastic capsule and remembering I'm guilty of killing somebody is jarring. I want to stop existing here and disappear back into my dream world; this horrible place holds no incentive for me to choose it over the lake, but no amount of closing my eyes and wishful thinking changes anything.

I assume it's morning. There's no light in here other than the ghostly glow of the vibrating handset. I answer and Esther's voice seems to fill the whole capsule, like she's crammed in here with me. "Nicholas, where are you? I got here as early as I could! What are you doing? I'm outside your apartment; I've been ringing your doorbell for ages! Let me in!"

I try to push myself up but bang my head on the wall, reminding me of precisely how small the capsule is. Stifling my cry, I whisper, "Esther, I'm so glad you called! I'm not at home, I'm at the capsule hotel next to your station. Be at your place in half an hour." I hang up and realise how abrupt I may have sounded. It's not like me. I hope Esther will understand.

She does understand. All of it. This is somewhat surprising, particularly as I only expect to tell her a half-truth: that I'm not entirely confident I'm going to Euchaea and that "if anything happens to me", I want her to know that I've always valued and appreciated her friendship. I spend the entire half hour before going to my good friend's apartment psyching myself up to meet her and rehearsing how I can tell her I'm going to kill myself without actually saying I'm going to kill myself. There's always a chance she might see past my words to what I'm really intending, but I have to take the risk. After all, I've postponed death and evaded the police for this. But once we get inside the apartment and I get talking, just as always happens when I speak to Esther, the truth spills out unreservedly. I want to shut up and wipe the terrible truths I'm confessing to her from her memory, but all of the details of yesterday: my walk to work, the confrontation with Nishi, the gun, the blood, Minamoto, the suicide attempt, Kato, the police, everything pours out of me as though the valve to stop them is broken and I have no control over my words.

I can almost see her paling right in front of me as I reach the point of telling her I've killed someone, and as she clasps her hands to her face, gasping, I even fear she might faint. But as I tell her of my failed attempt to kill myself, and my waning but still present intent to go through with it, it seems to flick a switch in her: the shocking, wilting woman is suddenly gone and Esther launches herself at me like a ferocious animal. She grabs me by the shoulders and screams at me, violently shaking me as though she's trying to dislodge the idea from my mind. And it truly hurts. "What the hell were you thinking?" she roars. "Don't you dare ever think like that! Don't you even dare!"

I'm shocked, but I know I shouldn't be. Aside from Naomi, Esther is my absolute closest friend and here I am, telling her I'm deliberately going to harm myself, that I'm never going to see her again. I feel ashamed, not so much at having attempted suicide, but more at the thought that perhaps I haven't properly considered what I'm doing or what the repercussions of my suicide will be on those who'll miss me. But surely I have? Surely I've been through all of the positives and negatives already? This has been the only thing on my mind since lunchtime yesterday. Esther simply doesn't know how much I've agonised over this. But her reaction is striking, if somewhat obvious and justified. I'm the opposite to her: I'm naturally an analytical type and I've never been able to master the spontaneity that Esther has: reacting to the gut instinct; responding with instant raw determination. Maybe it's this over-analytical nature that's making this whole ordeal worse; it's certainly because of this nature why I'm still alive. So is it a good or a bad thing? Sometimes I wish I wouldn't paralyse myself by so much thought. True, Esther doesn't know all of the angles I've tried to consider, but they're not important to her: she knows I shouldn't kill myself, and that's all there is to it. Part of me wants to embrace her opinion entirely, part of me thinks *'I knew I shouldn't have told her anything'*, but either way, I've upset her more than I've ever upset anyone and I'm too embarrassed now to look her in the eye. She grabs my head with both hands and forces me to face her. "Look at me!" she cries. "You don't dare even think about killing yourself, Nicholas! Look at me! Don't you dare!" Her grip is strong but I can feel her trembling. As I look at her, I see that she's only just managing to stop herself from shedding tears.

What have I done? I've never seen Esther cry or come even close to tears before. I should have expected this; I should have avoided this; but I needed to see her. Even so, seeing her or not, if I kill myself, it will still hit her the same way. The last thing I want to do is hurt her so badly. "I'm sorry," I try to whisper, but I can't quite muster the strength to get the words out clearly. "I'm so sorry."

Esther pulls me to her and hugs me so tightly it soon becomes almost difficult to breathe, but I don't say anything. I understand.

We spend the next few hours talking over numerous refills of tea. We reminisce about our younger days, adventures we had both with Naomi and before we knew her, and scrapes we got into, mostly caused by Esther. It's so nice to be distracted, at least for a short time, from the nightmare I'm living. But soon we're back to discussing my predicament. We go over everything I've already considered plus a few new ideas, but despite the gravity and the underlying hopelessness of our subject, I have to admit that I don't feel quite as despairing as I did yesterday. I'm genuinely surprised at the extent to which it helps to have a friend with me who cares and who voices her gut reaction, and it also reaffirms how much I appreciate Esther and how much I miss this quality in Naomi too. Despite this however, I'm still no nearer to a positive resolution, and I occasionally discourage myself, commenting that Esther can afford to think positively as she isn't the one going to The Terror. Each time I do this, she very kindly tells me off and helps me to refocus on searching for positive probabilities.

The proposal to admit my guilt and give myself up to the police surfaces a number of times and a curious thing happens each time. Although I don't understand why this is so, every time the suggestion is put forward, it seems just a fraction more appealing, given the completely hopeless circumstances: maybe it's because I'm discussing it with a positive person now and not just with my negative self. I still very much doubt I'll take that option, but perhaps if it comes up often enough, I may eventually start to think it's a good idea. Returning to the subject of the police also reminds me that as it's around lunch time, I've now been officially missing for twenty-four hours, and therefore the police may search for me in earnest. Almost in a panic, I grab my phone out of my pocket and switch it off, just in case they now decide to try calling me. As the phone falls dormant, I feel like I've just defused a ticking bomb. I think I even smile, though this could just be in my mind.

Esther brings me back to focus on our discussion with a deft stab at positivism, seeing as I'm undoubtedly going to latch onto the fact that I'm now officially being sought by the authorities. She suggests that if I do give myself up, although the police may not be too merciful, perhaps the Harvest Light will look kindly on my admission as a true sign of regret and somehow reduce my sentence. It's quite a nice thought but not a very realistic one: there's no probation or parole in The Terror.

Aware we're starting to stray into wishful thinking territory, we take a break and go out to the balcony for some fresh air. It's still hot outside but Esther's balcony faces away from the sun, mercifully providing us with shade. There's also a very slight breeze and as I close my eyes, the refreshing caress of the air moving across my face seems amplified. It feels wonderful, like nature itself is trying to calm me down, but now I start to wonder if I will ever feel a refreshing breeze in The Terror. Will I ever see the sun there? Will I ever have cause to smile or to feel refreshed or relieved ever again? I seem predisposed to negativity. Why can't I be more like Esther?

She suddenly gasps, grabs my arm and pulls me back inside. "I've got it!" she cries, trying to keep her voice low, but struggling equally to contain some mystery excitement. "I don't believe I didn't think of this before! Ken Ida! I've been thinking about this the wrong way all this time. I've been thinking just about you: what can you do? But Ken may be able to help. He's a friend of mine, we go back a few years, and he knows all sorts of crazy stuff. It might be a bit of a long shot, but I really think he could maybe come up with something!"

"You think he could maybe come up with something?" I repeat, and I'm almost certain my lack of enthusiasm has come across in my tone of voice, not that I mean it to. "You don't sound too sure. And what do you mean 'crazy stuff'? I'm not sure I need 'crazy stuff', I need a real solution!"

"Hey, you need help and this guy may be the one to help you! Look, we don't really have many options here. Actually, I think we've got none!" She has a point. "I'll give him a call. If he's home, we'll go over right now."

As Esther phones the crazy stuff-knowing Ken, I sit down again and suddenly realise I no longer have the urge to kill myself. It's gone. I don't exactly feel reinvigorated and full of new hope – still quite the opposite, in fact – but this time with Esther seems to have completely eradicated the notion of suicide. It's a startling and slightly confusing turnaround but I think I welcome it. I don't want to dwell on this too much however; if it's not going to be an option, I should try to put it out of my mind. But what else do I have to think about? This Ken person? I was wary of being conned by Tristan Kato the salesman last night (though I feel fairly certain now he wasn't trying to sell me anything), so with this even shorter time I now have left, I have no desire to spend it chasing crazy ideas. I've learned, all too late it seems, that every minute is important. I start to tell Esther I'm having second thoughts but she doesn't hear me.

"He's home," she smiles, excitedly. "I'll call a taxi."

I wonder if this friend of hers is a criminal, seeing as he knows lots of "crazy stuff" that might help me, a man trying to escape the terrible thing he's done. "Who is this guy anyway?" I'm not really sure I want to hear the answer, but the question has been asked, so I add, "What does he do?"

"Insurance," Esther replies, dialling for the taxi. "Claims investigations, things like that. He's a good guy, you'll like him – you'll probably like him."

"What?" For a moment, I want to question her further but she's already talking to the taxi company.

13
A Regrettable Lunch.

Esther recommends that I only use the special taxis with human drivers from now on. Navi-pods are everywhere but they take video and Rice Grain readings of each passenger to eliminate fraud and fare-dodging, so conceivably every journey I take could be monitored. Human-driven taxis, like cash, are a hark back to times gone by, another working link with tradition: the driver trusts that the passenger will pay, the passenger trusts that the driver knows where he's going (though it's actually considered something of a loveable quirk if the driver makes a navigational mistake) and no video or Grain records are taken, unless you want to pay with your Grain. They're a deliberate experience of simpler times, but they're expensive.

There's no conversation in the fifteen-minute taxi ride to Ken Ida's apartment. To prevent the taxi driver from getting even a hint of what's going on, we decide before the taxi arrives to talk about absolutely anything except what we're off to do; and so we sit in uncomfortable silence for the whole journey. If the circumstances were different, I have no doubt Esther would easily find something interesting to talk about, but even though I can see in her face a hint of optimism at what Ken Ida might be able to do for me, I can also tell all of this is weighing heavily on her. Every now and again, she stops staring out at the other sky lanes or at the streets below, and gives me a smile. I'm sure it's supposed to be a reassuring one, but she looks nervous, like she's on her way to an important job interview. There's nothing I can do to help her. It feels like over the past twenty-four hours, I've been finding new ways to plumb the depths of discomfort, and now I've reached a brand new low. I'm on my way to confess my horrific accidental crime to someone I've never met, based solely on Esther's recommendation. I trust her, but explaining everything to a complete stranger doesn't feel right. I feel more exposed. I feel *guiltier.*

The taxi sets down at the foot of an eight-storey apartment building in quite an upmarket area. I've never been here before. The streets are wide, there's an abundance of tall trees and clusters of individually designed detached houses dotted amongst the array of apartment complexes. Each detached house even appears to have its own front garden and parking spaces, though they're not like the beautiful garden of the house opposite my own modest apartment. These gardens seem to be more about size and status rather than energy-giving compact landscapes. The apartment building we're parked beside looks very stylish and very expensive, though not quite as stylish or expensive as many of the others around it. I assume it must have been built first, or it's the cheaper, less fussy alternative to the extremely high standard in this area. Either way, Ken Ida obviously does well for an insurance claims investigator.

Rather than using the building's intercom to let him know we've arrived, Esther phones Ken directly and he remotely unlocks the doors to let us up to the top floor. I don't know if I'm supposed to be reading anything into this. On the way up, I wonder what his apartment will look like: a well-to-do insurance claims investigator who knows lots of "crazy stuff" and who might be able to aide a fugitive from the law isn't the type of person I usually have any dealings with. Still, when we arrive, I'm quite surprised to see lots of unidentifiable parts from electronic gadgets strewn around his floor and a pile of unwashed dishes next to the kitchen sink as we pass by. There's also a large, framed movie poster on the wall for an acclaimed police film I suddenly remember I wanted to see and never got around to. Ken himself has long black hair with faded traces of copper or brown streaks, tied into two ponytails, one at the back and one near the top of his head, and he has the beginnings of a moustache. He looks a little older than me but bows humbly to greet us as we come in and apologises for the mess, explaining that he's in the middle of repairing some item I've never heard of, and needs parts from a number of other items I've also never heard of. I feel this might be a positive thing; the more he knows about things I know nothing about, the more chance he may know something Esther and I haven't considered. He clears a space for us to sit down on the sofa and offers us some tea, and once it's steeping in the pot, he invites us to explain what the problem is. He seems to be quite a nice man.

It isn't easy for me to talk about the events that have led up to this 'interview'. It would be a difficult thing to do even if I were talking to another close friend, but to this stranger, I find it hard to speak at all. This being the case, I'm grateful for Esther's occasional prodding and interjection; it calms the atmosphere and reminds me that this is a friend helping a friend, rather than a defence of the accused. Ken is visibly saddened when he hears about the accidental killing but he's strangely, almost unnaturally, calm as he questions me. He wants to know exactly where I was when the incident occurred, why I thought I might be able to get away with it, why I decided to commit suicide, why I've now changed my mind. Some questions are much harder to answer than others. He also asks a number of other things about my background that are thankfully much easier to answer and which Esther and I do as honestly as we can. It seems Esther's confidence in him may be instilling in me some confidence in him too as I find it gradually easier to open up to him. I even unbutton my suit jacket and show him the bloodstains on my shirt. It feels like such a long time since I last saw them and looking at them again brings the horror of the killing back to life. I see the struggle and the gun and the little red eruption that gradually spreads and spreads. It's even more vivid now than when I explained the incident to Ken only minutes ago. Seeing my obvious distress, Ken kindly offers me a clean T-shirt, which I put on immediately. He and I are about the same size so it's an okay fit. When we finally finish explaining everything, Ken sits back and after seeming to ponder for some time, he smiles and says, "You're in pretty serious trouble."

I tense up suddenly, a surprising anger rising from inside me, and I almost find its force frightening. How can this man be so flippant about something so serious and so terrible? Nice man or not, I want to shout at him, but somehow I manage to stop myself from saying anything.

"Yes, it's serious," Esther says, calmly, "So if you've got any ideas…"

"I've already got an idea," Ken says. "Unfortunately it doesn't come with a guarantee, but it's the only thing I can see having any chance of working. And it's pricey."

As suddenly as my anger appeared, it leaves me, and now I'm tense with anticipation. A new idea? "What is it?" I blurt out, unintentionally pushy. "Is there a way to escape Harvest?"

"I never said that," Ken answers. "I don't even know if that's possible, and I know a lot of things! Forgive me if I sound arrogant."

"What is it then?" both Esther and I say at the same time.

An even broader smile spreads across Ken's face as he begins to explain. He clearly loves what he does. "Have you ever heard of a *wrap*?" he asks.

I shake my head and notice Esther is shaking hers too.

"It's what some people use to try and commit fraud, or sometimes theft. Basically, it's a 'mask' for your Rice Grain. A good wrap is like a conductive film that covers the whole Grain and distorts or tries to conceal your identity or hide selected information. They can be reasonably effective, depending on the technology and on what you're trying to achieve. I know of people who've used them to create entirely new IDs too. Again, depending on what you're aiming to do, a wrap's effectiveness can be pretty decent or just so-so. The Rice Grain is far too complex for any wrap to be perfect though. It's hard enough just trying to track down and conceal physical data stored on it; the intangible stuff that the Harvest Light seems to read is still a complete mystery."

"Are you going to get to an up-side?" Esther interrupts.

I have to agree with her. "I don't want to sound ungrateful," I add, "but you don't sound like you think this has even the slightest chance of working."

"Steady, you two," Ken says, still smiling. "Let me finish. The whole Harvest process is a complicated thing! Harvestees have tried different types of wrap in the past, like ones for hiding specific crimes or for making completely new IDs, but they've all still been taken away. Of course, there's no way for us to know if their wraps were effective or not, but personally I don't think so. The technology wasn't good enough. And there are theories that it's not just the

Rice Grain that the Light reads but also the corresponding Ward Registration Card, the person's DNA, and their nanobots, so that it can still pluck them away even if the Grain says they're someone else. But this is all speculation. Plus we think the Light is powerful enough to see through any wrap that's been produced up to the last Harvest anyway, no matter how good it was thought to be at the time.

"But technology has moved on a lot in the past seven years. And I really do mean a lot. I'm suggesting we use a new type of wrap and a new way of thinking. Now we can make one that won't just cover your Grain completely but will also constantly bombard it with disruptive signals, hopefully making it almost unreadable. It certainly won't be read by conventional machines, but I guess the Harvest Light is the real test. On top of the disruptive layer, we have multiple layers of a fake ID and life history, which'll be generated by a computer. As for your DNA and nanobots, there's no way we can effectively alter those readings in such a short time but we can generate the ID for a very close relative of Nicholas Machida based on the same DNA, and use it as an ID for your wrap. If it's true that the Harvest Light reads DNA, then the theory is that no one can fool it by trying to become someone else completely. However, if we make you someone who's almost an exact match for Nicholas Machida, you'll probably still be taken, but as long as we give your new ID a good history, you should go to Euchaea. One final thing you'll have to do is go to the country. Some studies suggest that the Harvest Light is weaker as it gets to the end of its run outside of the city. This could be because the country's not as densely populated, it could just be that the Light doesn't have to work so hard, or maybe the power just tails off there, we don't know. Either way, any information can be useful information, so going as far out as you can, as close to the edge of the Harvest field as possible, might increase your chances."

At one stage in his spiel, things had sounded promising. Ken's enthusiasm, a 'new type of wrap and a new way of thinking', disrupting the real Grain's signal and covering it with a new one: I must admit, they gave me some hope. But hope fades quickly. There was a lot of supposition in what he said, a lot of ifs and maybes and 'hoping this will work out'. In some way, I suppose I'm grateful Ken hasn't tried to market the idea as foolproof, only for me to discover too late that it doesn't actually work, but I was honestly hoping for something more, something reassuring. "So, you're not actually sure this will work?" I say to him.

"You're Esther's friend so I'm being totally honest with you. No, I'm not one hundred per cent sure. There's never any way to be sure. Look, the fact is no one completely understands the Rice Grain and the Harvest Light, and if the day ever comes that we get even close to properly figuring them out, I can almost guarantee there'll suddenly appear a whole catalogue of new problems we never even considered before. It's like they've been designed not to be understood." His mouth turns upward slightly. I know he's trying to make a joke but he really shouldn't bother. "This wrap will work with the machines we use every day," he says, "but the Harvest Light is on a whole different level. The inescapable truth, Mr. Machida, is that this is a risk."

I can't do it. As I stand up, I realise I've said this out loud. But it's true. "I really can't. I've only got one chance at this and you can't assure me that there's any point at all in trying this wrap thing. This is madness."

"I hope you're not starting to get cross with me, Mr. Machida," Ken says. He's looking serious now. "You don't have to have my help. If you want, I can point you in the direction of my dad. He's priest at a shrine near here. If you give him lots of money, he'll give you some lucky charms, spend a couple of minutes chanting, and then hope for the best. There's your other option."

Esther stands too and takes my arm, trying to calm me down. "Come on, Nick," she says, softly. "What choice do we have? And besides, Ken's always like this. Even if the wrap was ninety-nine point nine per cent effective, he'd still say there were a million things that needed fixing on it."

"I'm not that bad," Ken objects. "But yes, there would still be a lot to address."

"See? Look, Nick, it's this or nothing. Okay, so it's not exactly my life on the line here, but I'd go for the wrap."

Gut reaction. My gut reaction is somewhere between "no" and "maybe not", but what are the alternatives? I have to do something. "I don't really have a choice, do I?"

"There's always a choice," says Ken. "What's it going to be?"

'It could work,' I think. *'Masking my own Rice Grain, having a different identity. True, there'll be no definite way to know if it works until the end, but my only other option is to do nothing. Hell, this isn't a choice at all.'* "Okay, I'll do it," I eventually sigh. "I might as well cover my bases."

"Good man," says Ken, smiling again. "I'll get the computer to start generating an ID. That's thirty-four years' worth of tiny details so it'll to take a few hours. In the meantime, I'm going to need three things if this is to have any hope of working: a sample of blood, your Ward Registration Card, and payment in cash. Sorry but this isn't going to be cheap."

My heart sinks. It's not that I've forgotten this could cost me an awful lot of money; with all that's been happening, money doesn't feel quite so important to me anymore anyway. No, it's that I now realise that because of ducking out to lunch early yesterday, my all-important Ward Registration Card is still in my wallet, my wallet is still in my briefcase, and my briefcase is still under my desk at the office.

14
The Weather Theory.

I can't simply return to work and collect my briefcase. Aside from the inevitable interrogation from my bosses and work colleagues, and a slight lingering personal shame at not having given a farewell speech, I'll most definitely be kept there until the police arrive to question me. Now that I've obviously been flagged up as a suicide risk, they'll want to talk to me about my Harvest and about why I temporarily disappeared. If that happens, although I'm still hopeful they have no reason to ask me anything about Nishi, it just isn't worth the risk of letting anything slip. I can't guarantee that I won't break down like a terrified child and confess to everything I've done if the police so much as ask me my name. I can't send Esther either: only DBDM employees and, in extreme emergencies, close relatives, are allowed beyond public areas, and even if she were to remain outside, she wouldn't be authorised to handle employee's personal effects. I guess I can understand some of the reasoning behind having such strict regulations, but right now they're only serving to make my life even more difficult and I could do without them. I consider whom I might be able to call and ask to meet Esther or me somewhere off-site with the case but all of my work colleagues' first duty is to the Department. If I call anyone, at the very least they'll inform my department head of what they're doing. It isn't betrayal, it's simply the responsible thing to do; this is how we or anyone else would show concern for the wellbeing of our colleagues. If the situation were reversed, I know I'd do the same. Suddenly Minamoto springs to mind. I'm not sure why, I've only known the man one day, but he seems trustworthy and able to keep a secret – at least he did yesterday morning when I broke down in front of him. Or perhaps I'm mistaking trustworthiness for a not-yet-ingrained loyalty to the Department. Either way, I have to admit I didn't feel as out of line expressing some of my distress to him yesterday as I would have done had it been to anyone else at the office. And it's not as though I'm going to tell him I've killed someone either; I'm just going to ask him to meet one of us with my briefcase.

Esther makes a voice-only call to the DBDM and asks for Minamoto, and as he answers, I take over. He's curious as to why I'm making a non-visual call to work but I tell him I'm not dressed and don't wish to speak to the department head because I neglected my duties to the department yesterday. After a half-fabricated story about some important documents I've left at the office, he's happy to meet me with my briefcase at the coffee shop of the Kettei Company Building where I met Kato the salesman yesterday evening. He's uncomfortable at the notion of handing over the case to a stranger and although I try, he can't be convinced to make the exchange with Esther instead, so I concede to meet him in person. On the bright side, he isn't troubled about not mentioning any of this to his work colleagues and so we agree to meet in an hour.

Despite the fact that I'm in a taxi, flying high above the streets, I still feel like I'm 'out in the open' in the centre of the city and I don't like it at all. Other cars, some of them police cars, fly alongside us occasionally and I try to discreetly hide my face. A police officer might recognise me (if they're looking for me), or someone else from the office might spot me (somehow) and notify work or the police directly. I can see the forty-nine-storey Kettei Building from some way off and I hope Minamoto is waiting outside so I won't have to get out of the taxi, but as the vehicle lands, I can't see him. I now wish Esther was here to go inside instead of me. Rather than accompany me however, she has stayed at Ken's place to rehearse the Rice Grain 'wrapping' procedure. After our phone conversation with Minamoto, Ken explained that the process can't be done in only one-stage and it will be up to Esther to make sure it's done properly. I actually ended up insisting that she stay back with Ken to practice as much as she can. I really can't afford any mistakes.

As my own phone has to remain switched off in case the police try to call me, I have Esther's phone with me instead, and I sit with my thumb nervously pressed to the screen, wondering if I should call Minamoto and ask him to come out to the idling taxi with my briefcase. It's almost a whole minute before any sense returns to me and I remember I don't have Minamoto's direct number anyway. There's no way I can call him even if I want to. The taxi driver eyes me in the mirror, presumably wondering why I'm still sitting here, staring at the coffee shop window, so I tell him to wait for me and I head inside. I know nobody's really noticed me as I walk in – to them I'm just another customer seeking refuge from the oppressive heat outside – but it feels like they're all watching me. I wish I could become invisible and I even find myself wondering if that's possible if I concentrate hard enough. The stress must be driving me insane – insane enough to try it. But I soon know it hasn't worked because there's someone in the far corner of the shop waving me over. It's Minamoto.

"Machida!" he beams as I get to him. "It's good to see you."

I wish he'd keep his voice down, but at the same time I'm surprised at how relieved I am to see him again. I'm not sure why this is; I wasn't expecting to feel anything at all but it's almost like meeting up with an old friend – an old friend who hopefully has my briefcase.

"You had some of us worried when you didn't return to work yesterday," he says. "You were so upset, I thought maybe you'd gone and thrown yourself under a train or something."

I try to smile slightly at Minamoto's attempt at humour but it makes me so uncomfortable to know how close he is to the truth. "Good to see you too," I reply. "Sorry I caused some concern at work. Maybe it was a mistake not to go back yesterday, but I just had lots on my mind: the Harvest and everything."

"Don't worry about it," Minamoto says. "I took over your workload anyway so that's all taken care of. What else are you worrying about?"

'Where do I begin?' I'm aching inside and a part of me almost wants to pour out to Minamoto what the real problem is. *'If only you could take over* that *load too!'* "Just stuff. All the things I've done, all the mistakes I've ever made. Y'know, the usual Harvest worries."

Minamoto points out of the window. "Look outside, Machida."

I follow his finger but there's nothing unusual there. Just my waiting taxi.

"The sun's shining," he says. "Even if you've spent your whole life making mistakes, when you walk out that door, the sun's still going to shine. However much you worry, or whatever you've done, it's not going to change that fact. The Harvest is the same: you can change your Harvest by worrying about your mistakes just as much as you can change the weather by worrying about your mistakes, so don't worry. You're not perfect and the Harvest knows that. It won't punish you for your mistakes. What matters is what you do about those mistakes. Do you want a coffee?"

It takes me a moment to realise he's asked me a question. "Sorry, I can't stay, I've got a taxi waiting outside. I told him I'd only be a minute."

"Pity. Are you going away somewhere?"

"Just out to the country maybe. Y'know, spend my final couple of days having a proper break."

"Good plan. Rumour has it the Harvest Light isn't so strong out there."

I tense up but I'm hoping it doesn't show. "What? What do you mean?" Surely Minamoto can't have guessed I'm attempting to escape my Harvest. I try not to rub the base of my skull.

"Well, that's the rumour, isn't it?" says Minamoto, still smiling. "Less scary: softer. No matter how many times you see a Harvest, it's always kinda frightening: just that infinite wall of light as far as you can see, and that deep humming sound that vibrates right through you. People say that in the country, it's a less frightening thing, that's all. Maybe that's because it's not vibrating off all these buildings, maybe it's because the air's less dense, who knows. You've never heard that before?"

"No." Minamoto's explanation seems innocent but I'm still on my guard. "No, I've never heard that. I'm just going. With a friend."

"Well, I hope you have a good time. Have you been to the country before?"

"Just once, years ago, but not to the end. Have you got my briefcase? I really do have to go."

Minamoto reaches down and hands the case over. "After you didn't come back, it got moved to the department head's office. Talk about 'cloak and dagger' getting it out of there! Don't worry though, nobody knows it's gone – not yet. And I'm glad we got to meet up again anyway, even if it was just for a minute or two. Have a great time in the country, and I hope to see you in Euchaea one day. If there's anything you need before Harvest, give me a call." He hands me his name card. "But if you leave it until after Harvest, it'll be too late." He grins again.

"Oh, I never gave you my card," I apologise and start to fumble with my case to find one.

"Don't worry about it," Minamoto says. "I work for the DBDM now, we know everything."

It's one of the departmental jokes of the DBDM that with all of the information we process, nothing in the city escapes our knowledge. As I leave the building, taking special note of the glorious sun above me that hasn't stopped shining despite what I've done, I'm so glad that it really is just a joke.

15
The Flightless Bird.

The city is usually claustrophobic, but I'm inclined to describe it as a 'comfortable claustrophobia': the 'crammed-in' nature of everything from the buildings to the people is normal fair, and I daresay that everyone and everything being so close even aids the stability of our society. We keep each other in check, we're answerable to everyone; this can sometimes make life hard or a little unforgiving, but in the end, harmony is everyone's responsibility. Sometimes claustrophobia is good. Conversely, I've never experienced agoraphobia before, but I have a feeling it may be similar to what I'm experiencing now. I've asked the taxi driver to land so that I can access a convenient Teller Point and withdraw the cash for Ken, but standing out in the open, I feel like a vulnerable little animal, somehow lost and far away from the safety of its natural habitat. The ground vehicles passing by me seem over-sized and loud and dangerous; every person is glancing at me, wondering if I'm the man who killed Jon Nishi; they're hovering by their phones, poised to call the police if I make eye contact with any of them. The towering buildings, once so tightly packed together, are all now deliberately spaced out to allow an even greater number of people to stare at me and single me out when the police arrive. The towers start to sway as the heated breeze blows through them and the city itself begins to roll and lurch. My legs are weakening so I close my eyes and hold onto the side of the Teller Point until the motion stops. This place is killing me; I need to get out of here.

I hear a soft bleep from the Teller Point and slowly open my eyes. The movement has stopped and my legs feel largely back to normal again. Whatever it was seems to have passed. My details have appeared on the screen and I suddenly experience a sense of impending loss. If what Ken is doing works, this will be the last time I see myself as Nicholas Machida. Soon, this man will no longer exist in the eyes of the city, the police, and hopefully the Harvest. It's an odd and not exactly pleasant feeling. I'm prevented from dwelling on it however, as I'm also suddenly aware that if there are any police alerts for the use of my Rice Grain, they'll now know where I am. I quickly withdraw the cash, get back into the taxi and head off.

I'll miss me, but perhaps the world will improve without me. Nicholas Machida only seems to be the cause of pain and difficulty lately so perhaps if I no longer exist, things will be better. Whether or not the Harvest Light will agree that I don't exist anymore, I doubt there will be any way to tell for sure until the very end. Unfortunately, by that time, if there are any flaws in the plan, it will be too late to do anything about it. There's just too much uncertainty in all of this and it's making me more and more nervous. Ken told me that staying calm and not raising my adrenaline too much should help the wrap settle onto my Rice Grain more effectively. But how can I possibly be calm? If only there was some way to be sure: some way to really hedge my bets. I pull out Kato the salesman's business card and tell the taxi driver to land again. I'm sure he's getting a little bit annoyed at this starting and stopping; he doesn't sigh or argue but I can see his frown in the mirror. I ask him to wait for me while I get out and make a call, and this time when we land, I crouch by a wall to prevent the city from spinning. There's no time to meet up with the salesman now, but if he has any last minute ideas, I'm all for trying.

Kato doesn't look at all surprised to see me. I don't even have to remind him who I am as he launches straight into a question. "So, Mr. Machida, have you come up with a new idea for delaying your Harvest?"

I immediately put the phone up to my ear so that no one else can hear him. I hope no one heard what he's already said. "What are you doing?" I almost hiss, "Someone could have heard you!"

"Sorry, I didn't know it was such a big secret." He doesn't sound very repentant. "So, any new ideas?"

I'm already a little disappointed. "No. Actually, I'm calling to ask if you've had any flashes of inspiration."

"Not really. I did go to a priest this morning though. I paid him some money and he gave me a lucky charm and chanted for a while."

"Someone said the same thing to me today. Do you feel any better?"

"I don't feel any different if that's what you're asking, but at least it's done and checked off. Listen, if you're really that concerned, I'm sure there are ways. And you're not up for Harvest yet anyway, right, so you've got at least another seven years and three days to think of something."

I'm not sure why I keep up the pretence that I'm not already a Harvestee, but I reply, "Yes."

"Well I don't have seven years and three days," Kato says, "I have three days, so I've got to get moving."

"Wait a second. If your name's already been called, how can you still delay your Harvest? It's already been determined that you're going."

"When *delay* is no longer the name of the game, it becomes *escape*."

My stomach feels as though it's leaped. "You're going to try and escape? How?" I need to hear this.

"Sorry, I can't tell you that. Some secrets should stay secret. And besides, I hardly know you. You could be a Harvest Agent and haul me up on charges of attempting to pervert the natural course of Harvest. Then I'd really be in trouble." He laughs but I can tell he's serious.

"I'm not a spy!" I protest. "The only thing I have to do with the government is that I work for the Department for Births, Deaths and Marriages."

"Harvest Agents don't work for the government. They work for the Harvest."

Kato is starting to sound flippant; the Harvest Agents he's referring to are justice-dealing spirits of urban myth, as old as 'The Scrutiny of Harold Kanagawa', and it's actually a little difficult for me not to get angry with him. I find it hard to believe that even Kato's obsession to 'hedge his bets' goes that far. "I don't work for the Harvest either!" I try to calm down. This is far too important for me to lose my temper and risk pushing Kato away. "But seriously, if you've got an escape plan, I'd really love to hear it."

"No can do, I'm afraid. I wouldn't want to risk anything being jeopardised."

"Jeopardised?" What can I possibly say or do to make Kato tell me? If there's any other chance at all for avoiding Harvest, I simply have to know. "I thought you were a salesman," I try, "Aren't you supposed to attempt to sell me something? Sell me an idea. I'll pay." I wonder if telling him I'm willing to pay sounds too desperate; but I *am* desperate. I just don't want him to know.

"Not even birds fly all the time," Kato replies. "Today, Mr. Machida, I'm very much on the ground."

'Birds?' This isn't working. Perhaps I can be honest with him: tell him I'm also a Harvestee and tell him my own plan for escape; maybe he might open up to me. For a second, I think it's worth a try but the more I think about it, the more I find I'm also unable to open up. Telling Kato about the wrap and the countryside isn't going to alter my plans (at least I don't think so), but it doesn't feel *safe* to let others in on what I'm doing. It'll only make me feel even more vulnerable if I tell him, and I can barely cope as it is. Now I understand what he means: I don't want to risk anything being jeopardised either.

"I tell you what," Kato continues. "Remember the coffee shop where we met yesterday? I'll leave the details for you with a member of staff there on Harvest morning. You can go and get it after Harvest. I know it all sounds very 'spy-like' but I just can't risk telling you before I go and having others find out. I don't want people getting in the way. After the Harvest, you can think it over and then decide whether or not you want to try it too. Deal?"

This is a disaster. I'm so close to another possible means of escape, one that this man seems reasonably confident about, but I'm not being granted access – not until it will be too late. But still I can't tell Kato that I intend to be far away from the city when the Harvest comes, that there will be no way for me to make use of the information he's proposing to leave for me. "But what if the staff read your plan?" I almost plead, attempting to convince him of the need to change his mind. I already know it's a feeble attempt.

"I'll put it in a storage cylinder and tell them it's for you. It's okay, they won't open it."

"You can't be sure."

"It's a risk. But life's full of risks, just ask any salesman – or any bird. Do we have a deal?"

I sigh, really quite angrily. I want to argue more but I know there's no point. "Yes, it's a deal."

"Excellent," Kato says. I can almost tell that he's smiling again. "Cheer up, Mr. Machida. Just relax. It won't do you any harm to do nothing until after the Harvest. Enjoy the festivities, or take some time out to relax. I hear the countryside's nice."

I'm really not in the mood. "Yeah, I hear that too," I tell him. "Well, good luck with your plan. If you change your mind and decide it's okay to let me know before Harvest morning, call me back." I give him Esther's number and my own, just in case. Desperate times.

"You're a good man, Mr. Machida," says Kato. "Who knows, maybe we'll meet again somewhere. In the meantime, enjoy the Harvest! See you around." He hangs up, and with him disappears any new hope of escape. I can't handle this. I'm beginning to feel the unbearable tugs of depression again so I try to refocus. I already have an escape plan: I'm not particularly comfortable with it, but it's my only option. I shouldn't waste any more time thinking about Kato and his bird metaphors. Three days: I need to get moving too.

16

The Discourteous Second Disappearance of Nicholas Machida.

Much to the taxi driver's relief, I imagine, he drops me off back at Ken Ida's stylish apartment building. After having made him wait a number of times, and all of the starting and stopping, I now feel bad that I'm paying cash for the journey too. In an attempt to lessen the over all inconvenience I've been to him, I tell him to keep the change. He bows in his seat and says, "Thank you", but he doesn't smile and I don't blame him.

Ken has given me strict instructions not to use the building intercom but to call him directly when I arrive. He claims this is a precaution against easy tracking, should it become necessary at any time to erase any traces of he and I ever having had any contact. This doesn't exactly give me confidence in the endeavour, but I suppose if someone like Ken is going to be involved in matters that aren't always law-abiding, a measure of paranoia is only to be expected. I make the call, the doors are unlocked, and I return to the top floor where I'm greeted with an uncustomary handshake from Ken and a very welcome hug from Esther.

"What was that for?" I ask her, grateful but confused.

Esther smiles. "Strange as it may sound, I was actually really worried for you while you were out. I think I might be turning into your mom."

I pay the money to Ken, and it's only now that I start to feel a little wary at handing over such a large sum of cash. I'm not certain why. Surely, with every hour that passes, money is becoming less and less valuable to me? Perhaps it's because the paying of so much money is symbolic of the heavy investment I'm making in this plan. Or more likely, perhaps the amount of money I'm putting in is merely cementing my criminality and my guilt. Still, the funds are paid and the process of replacing Nicholas Machida with a man who doesn't really exist begins.

The computer has concocted Michael Tamura, a cousin of Nicholas Machida from three wards away, the same age and very similar in appearance with a reasonably respectable office job. I can hardly believe I've paid so much for such an uncreative effort: I could have come up with something far more interesting myself in a fraction of the time, and for free. I don't know if it's the accumulating pressure I'm under that's making me speak up when previously I would have kept quiet, but I stop Ken as he's about to speak. "Michael Tamura? My cousin? Am I missing something here? When you said the computer needed to create an ID that's almost an exact match to me, I was thinking more like an identical twin or something like that. What's this all about?" I don't think I've come across as particularly angry, but even Esther seems surprised that I've been so forward with my opinion. But the really odd thing is that I don't feel even the slightest regret at doing so.

"Good," Ken says. He doesn't look cross at my questioning his work or that of his computer. "I'm glad you're thinking about this properly, asking the right questions. It'll help you to understand more about what you're doing and hopefully make this wrap more complete. We can't make you Nicholas Machida's twin because if we did, every time your wrap gets scanned, it'd immediately cross-reference every record of Nicholas Machida and show him with absolutely no trace of a twin brother. Your fake ID would be exposed instantly. However, with cousins, we have licence to be a little shadier. There's no first-instance direct cross-referencing to cousins when a Grain's scanned – it's just one of those bizarre things that nobody really knows the reason for – so we just mess with the family line a little, blur a relationship here or a liaison there, and then it's like Michael Tamura has always been around, and you don't set off any alarms. We're still very close to the original you, but we're standing just far enough away so as not to arouse suspicion, if you catch my meaning. Trust me, this is the best way to do it. And it's not easy putting something this insanely complicated together."

As Ken goes on explaining more about the need to have an ID different yet similar enough to my real one, I skim through some of the preliminary profile details and events currently moving up the display screen and begin to realise just how in depth the computer has actually gone. There are details here I would never have considered: at four years, three months and eleven days old, at exactly 14.05 on a day almost as hot as today, Michael Tamura accidentally dropped his ice cream on the pavement after he'd had only two licks. He didn't cry, but he'd wanted to, and he spent a good few hours angry at his older cousin (a real older cousin of mine), for making him pick up the wasted treat and dispose of it properly. He never told anyone that he later found a splash of ice cream on his shoe and licked it off. That tiny taste cheered him up for the rest of the day. As well as every exacting detail of the incident, each corresponding emotion is also listed, from the initial shock and helplessness to the distress and upset, the struggle not to cry, the anger and the sense of loss, the small triumph and the feeling of consolation. Sometimes it's a single word emotion, sometimes there are five or six. Absolutely nothing is missed. I'm even more astounded when I ask Ken what the line *'CONDITION: FADE / SUBJECT VALUE = NIL'* flashing under the ice cream incident means and he tells me it signifies that Michael Tamura doesn't even remember this particular thing happening; the Rice Grain, however, does. Now faster than I can read, the segment disappears off the screen, replaced by more events, hours later, days later, important and insignificant, remembered and forgotten, all of the emotions involved and the memories they trigger and cross-reference. There's so much information scrolling by, it's becoming one big blur. According to Ken, there isn't time to read what's there anyway as the massive section on display at the moment is less than one-thousandth of the information the computer has generated. It's a truly incredible piece of work: Michael Tamura's entire *life* up to Harvest Day in three days' time has been coded out, ready to be over-laid onto my Rice Grain. I think I'm starting to feel that this could actually work.

The first stage of my transformation, masking my Grain with a disruptive signal to make it unreadable, is done immediately. I'm directed to sit down and try to relax, which isn't easy, but it isn't quite as hard to do as I thought it would be either. I feel strange: it's like an emptiness – a nothingness – throughout my whole body, like I'm about to be executed but it's only something I'm observing rather than something that's actually happening. I don't feel fear, only anticipation.

Watched closely by Esther, Ken applies a warm translucent gel to the back of my head and neck, covering the vicinity of my Rice Grain. He connects a hand-held device to the computer and presses the device against the patch of gel, moving it up and down until it sounds a gentle *ping.* "Found your Grain," he says, and adds, "This might burn a little." As soon as he says it, I begin to feel an increasing heat seeming to originate from inside my skull, from where I believe my Rice Grain to be. It isn't exactly painful but it's one of the most uncomfortable, unnatural feelings I've ever experienced and I start to feel dizzy.

"I don't feel right," I say, wobbling slightly on my seat. Esther jumps forward and steadies me. "Am I supposed to be feeling dizzy? Are you sure this is safe, Ken?"

I hear him say something to Esther but I immediately forget what it is and say, "I think I'm going to be sick." About two seconds later, I throw up into a bowl that Esther is already holding in front of me. I now remember what Ken said to her just after I told him I was feeling dizzy: he told her to grab the bowl. I also notice he's kept the hand-held device pressed to the back of my head as I lurched over to vomit. I get the feeling he may have done this a number of times before. I only throw up the one time but the uneasiness stays with me and I feel only a little relieved when, after about ten minutes of constant heat inside my head and a slowly fading nausea and dizziness, Ken finally moves the device away. "Right," he smiles. "Now you're officially nobody."

"What?" I'm really not sure what I expected during this transformation. Did I think I was going to feel like a different person? Was I going to feel like I no longer exist (however that actually feels)? Whatever I might have expected, it was certainly more than a few minutes of dizziness and vomiting. "Is that it?" I ask, uncertain what else there should be.

"Not quite," says Ken. "That was just the disruptive wrap. That was the beginning. Now we need to give it some time to settle on your Rice Grain. After about five hours you'll be able to put on the first layer of your new ID without it interfering with the disruptive wrap or vice-versa."

"Five hours?"

"If you want this done properly, then yes, five hours. In the meantime, we'll do your Ward Registration Card. That'll only take a couple of hours, two-and-a-half at most. After that, it's all up to the two of you." He wipes the end of the device with a cloth, unplugs it from the computer, and carefully places it into a very small, specially moulded case. I can see there's a compact space in the moulding to house the folded up computer too. "I take it you'll be on a maglev out of here tomorrow morning," Ken continues, "so Esther will take the equipment and put the first of the Tamura ID layers on you this evening. I've already explained that she needs to apply five layers for best security and that you should wait four hours after administering one layer before putting on the next one. That way, each one has time to get cosy with its new host. It's straightforward enough so you shouldn't need to worry too much about it. And that, *Mr. Tamura*, is that."

'*That,* Mr. Tamura, *is that*'. I'm not quite sure what to say. This is the beginning of the end of my life as Nicholas Machida. In fact, in a sense that life has already ended; now I'm no one and this is the beginning of my life as somebody new: Michael Tamura. There are no words.

"I'll take that as a 'thank you'," says Ken.

"Of course, sorry." I realise my silence might have come across as rude. "Yes, thank you. Thanks so much for doing this. You have no idea how much I appreciate it."

Ken smiles at me, knowingly. "I think I can imagine."

Now I'm absolutely certain he's done this a number of times before.

17
Even People Who Don't Exist Can Fail.

I wonder what kind of people Ken has carried out Rice Grain wraps for. Maybe people like me: fugitives trying to escape the law or the Harvest? Con artists and fraudsters taking on temporary identities for elaborate thefts? Perhaps unscrupulous rising politicians looking to blot out misdemeanours from the past or enhance their apparent qualification for office? But it can't be only bad people who might have a Rice Grain wrap: what about good politicians simply wanting a fair chance to shine, not permanently tainted by pre-office mistakes? What about people under witness protection perhaps, or those escaping abusive partners? Innocent victims of circumstance: again, people like me? I wonder if any of those people are still here. Have their Harvests already been? Did those with completely new identities – those wanting to escape their Harvests or ensure one destination over the other – succeed in going where they wanted to go? Or if their wraps are intended for this coming Harvest, are those 'customers' of Ken's going through the exact same struggles as I am?

How does an insurance claims investigator end up involved in this kind of business?

Five hours after the beginning of my own transformation from Nicholas Machida to the fictional Michael Tamura, I still have a warm throbbing sensation inside my skull. It feels wrong. A Rice Grain is supposed to remain pure and untouched. Having it now bombarded with disruptive signals after thirty-four years of nothing and actually feeling it happen is unsettling to say the least. Still,

Ken did assure me that the process is completely harmless, so I'm trying my best to believe him. I wonder if his other customers believed him? I wonder if they can still feel the throbbing even now? Maybe I'm supposed to get used to it. Esther and I return to my apartment despite my severe apprehension. Sometimes I don't understand why it's so difficult for her to see my point of view. It's not unreasonable to believe that the police might be watching the place, waiting for me to come home, but Esther somehow convinces me (temporarily) that I'm being more paranoid than is necessary. On the way, it's a struggle I can barely contain not to grab her by the arm, drag her off the monorail, and flee back to her apartment instead. But I need to change clothes, I need to pack for the next couple of days, and if I feel it's necessary, I should put my apartment in order. I probably won't feel it's necessary at all, but some traditions are difficult to let go of. There are other things I know I'm supposed to be doing now: tying up my work affairs, paying up my rent, my bills, rounding off a billion things at the Ward Office, but I really don't care about any of that. The only important things now are getting my Rice Grain wrapped and ensuring Esther and I are on the maglev out of here tomorrow morning. If we can think of anything else that might aide my not to going to The Terror, I can add them to the list too, as and when.

I'm relieved to see no police outside my apartment when we arrive and there's no sign of anyone having been inside when we cautiously enter. I prevent the lights from switching on automatically until the front door is closed. I don't really know why. I feel like a thief breaking into my own home. Although there are no police physically present, my 'paranoia' is given some credibility when Esther sees that they've left me an intercom video message. It's one of the policemen I saw outside my apartment last night and he talks to the machine as though talking to me directly. He has a serious expression but he's speaking in a practiced, soothing yet authoritative tone, the way only police officers seem to be able to. He tells me the time and date he and his colleague were here, he says they've had concern from the DBDM due to my status as a Harvestee and my not returning to work and that he just wants to check on me, he wishes me well and informs me they'll try to contact me again. Hurriedly, I make sure my phone is still switched off. I was right about why the police were at my apartment last night but it doesn't make me feel any better.

After the message, Esther checks her watch again. She seems to have been doing so about every fifteen minutes since I had the disruptive Rice Grain wrap put on. "Hey, Mr. Nobody," she says with some urgency. "It's five hours. We should put the first layer of your ID on now."

I start to tell her I'd prefer to do it elsewhere, maybe at her apartment, but not here at mine; I want to grab only what I need to grab, sort only what I need to sort, and leave. But Esther argues that with five layers to apply and at least four hours between each layer, it's going to take at least sixteen more hours to complete, not including sleep time, so we need to make a start as soon as possible. I also get the feeling she's just as anxious about getting this process right as I am. I decide to relent: I may be uneasy about spending this extra time at my apartment, but the sooner we can make a start with this, the better I think we'll both feel.

Esther carefully unfolds the computer from its compact case and sits herself on the sofa so I pull up a cushion and sit on the floor in front of her. My paranoia, as Esther calls it, is overtaken by very real nervousness. I'm nervous about being at my apartment while the police are probably looking for me, even if it's just to 'check on me'. I'm nervous about the process of wrapping my Rice Grain: if something goes wrong, if it's not wrapped around my Grain perfectly, the consequences will be catastrophic. I'm nervous about becoming (or at least pretending to be) a completely different person; I know pretty much nothing about Michael Tamura. And I'm suddenly nervous about being *erased*: about me – the real me – Nicholas Machida, truly not existing anymore; all of my memories, my childhood adventures, my adult experiences, all covered up, deleted. Am I killing Nicholas Machida now? Am I doing something worse: not just cutting him off before his time, but denying all that he's ever been, all that he ever was to the people who know him? Am I doing the right thing? I have to stop questioning myself. I've been through the whole decision-making process already; that's why I'm here now, that's why I'm going through with this.

Esther interrupts my circular thoughts. "Remember, try to relax. Are you relaxed?"

I answer her honestly. "Not really."

She speaks softly and starts stroking the top of my head. "Ken said relaxing helps. And c'mon, Nick, at the very least, this first ID layer should be making you feel great. At the moment, you're the equivalent of an empty shell: you're like a walking body without a name or a life or a history. *That* is a bad situation to be in. Now we're going to put it right. So relax." She stops stroking and gently pats me on the shoulder.

I don't know how effective her reasoning has actually been but I experience quite a sudden shift away from my negative attitude when she very expertly sets the computer, applies the gel to the back of my head, connects the handset and calibrates it, holds the device to my skull, gets the confirming *ping* to signify she'd found the right spot, and starts the thirty-minute upload of information to my Rice Grain. She's learned such a lot from Ken in such a short time. It's true there are some things I'm nervous about but concern for whether or not this wrap is being done properly is suddenly no longer one of them.

In some way, I've actually started to develop some confidence in the plan. I'm not entirely comfortable with it – I can't get away from that – but I think some of Ken's enthusiasm has stealthily rubbed off on me. This really is amazing technology, the kind I've never seen before. If Ken is to be believed, I truly think this course of action may well be worth attempting (I can think it may well be worth attempting and still have serious doubts about it at the same time). I'm also trying not to think about Kato's mystery escape plan; that's none of my concern. However, I do wish I shared some of his apparent composure, or perhaps better still, some of Minamoto's optimism: the new DBDM employee always seems so positive about the Harvest. I wonder now if perhaps I should have told him my situation; maybe his positive outlook could have found other options for me. But it's too late for that. I'm committing to going through with the plan I've got, and that's all there is to it.

"Do you ever really wonder what Euchaea's like?" Esther suddenly asks, still holding the handset steady against the back of my head.

"I used to," I reply. "But, believe it or not, I'm actually trying not to think too much about it now. I don't know how this is all going to go, so I'd rather not focus on Euchaea, and on Naomi and my folks and all the things I may or may not see again."

"I hear you. But you've got to try and be positive. This is some of the best technology out there. And besides, I have my own theories about the Harvest and I don't think your situation is hopeless."

I want to turn to face her but I know I shouldn't move. "What do you mean?"

"Well, you killing Nishi was an accident. It was self-defence. If the Harvest is as clever as we all think it is, surely it'll know you didn't mean to do it; that it was a mistake. I don't think the Harvest punishes you for your mistakes."

"You sound like Minamoto. He was saying the same kind of thing when I picked up the briefcase from him. I had no idea you were so optimistic." For some reason, I'm smiling a little. Maybe it helps just to be around optimistic people.

"We're good friends, Nick, but I'm sure there's a lot you don't know about me. Anyway, as long as this wrap works, you won't need to worry."

Something unpleasant occurs to me. "But I'm doing this wrap on purpose. I'm deliberately trying to escape what's happened. If the Harvest Light sees through the false ID, surely it'll know *this* wasn't a mistake."

"And it'll know I deliberately helped you too. What does that mean for me?"

I never thought of that either: is Esther implicating herself by helping me? Before I can say anything, she adds, "Maybe it's just not always possible to know the right thing to do. Maybe we can only try and hope. I guess we have to hope that alongside all of that apparent intelligence, the Harvest Light also has mercy."

"Mercy? I don't think I have enough optimism for that."

"That's not optimism, that's hope. Optimism and hope aren't always the same thing."

The doorbell rings and we immediately fall silent. My heart begins to race; no one's supposed to know I'm home. Hopefully it's just a salesman or a neighbour; if we do nothing, perhaps they'll go away. For thirty seconds we sit completely still, completely silent, as though the slightest move we make or the quietest whisper might alert the person outside to our presence. It's excruciating. The bell rings again. This time, whoever is ringing also bangs on the door.

"Who the hell is that?" Esther whispers, as the person outside lifts the letterbox and shouts in, "Nicholas Machida. This is the police. Please open the door."

For a second, my heart feels like it's gone from panicked racing to a dead stop. What now? They know someone's home: they've certainly seen there's a light on inside the apartment and there's doubtless at least one officer already heading round to the rear of the building. We can't slip away.

"Mr. Machida!" the policeman shouts again.

"Damn it, I don't believe this!" I hiss. We're trapped. We have to let him in, there's no other choice. "This is madness! Hide the computer while I go and talk to him." I have no idea what I'm going to say.

Esther still has the handset pressed to the back of my head. "It hasn't finished uploading yet, it's still got eight minutes to go."

"We can't wait eight minutes! I have to open the door. Put the stuff back in the case and we'll sort it out later!" I leap to my feet and run out to the front door, stopping quickly at the kitchen sink to run my hair under the tap and wash off the gel. "Just a moment!" I shout whilst Esther clears the equipment away. This is acting with spontaneity, and it's making me feel sick.

"Nicholas Machida?" the policeman asks as I open the door.

"Yes," I answer. *'Damn it, no! My Grain's being masked. I'm not Nicholas Machida anymore!'* "Yes, this is Nicholas' apartment. But he isn't here. He's gone to the country for Harvest."

"Can I ask who you are?"

Who am I? I have to calm down; I have to think straight. "I'm Michael Tamura, Nicholas' cousin." *'I really hope I'm Michael Tamura, my cousin.'*

"And what are you doing here?" The other policeman comes round from the back of the building to join the first.

"Oh, I'm just getting some things for him," I say.

"I see. May we come in for a moment?"

To say anything other than "yes" will be hugely suspicious so I let them in and lead them to the living room where Esther is sitting watching TV. I introduce her and they politely bow. "Is something the matter?" she asks, innocently.

"That's what we want to find out," the first policeman says. I realise he's the same one from yesterday and from the intercom message. "Nicholas Machida left work at lunch time yesterday and didn't return. His Grain registered at a couple of places yesterday evening and then again this afternoon, withdrawing a large sum of money from a Teller Point, but he hasn't been back to work or to the Ward Office to close his affairs. We had a call from his place of employment yesterday after he didn't return, voicing some concerns for his safety. Is there anything you can tell us?"

"Well," I'm trying to think quickly, "He was in a bit of a state yesterday evening when I spoke to him. But I saw him this afternoon before he set off and he seemed much better then."

"What was the matter with him?"

"It was just the whole thing about being up for Harvest. He was getting really stressed about it so in the end he just wanted to get away from everything. He said he couldn't face coming back to the city, he just couldn't bear it anymore, so he asked us to take some things out to him tomorrow morning." The words are just spilling out of me and I'm not sure whether they sound convincing or utterly fake. Either way, I feel like I've put us in danger by telling the police we're planning to leave the city tomorrow morning. Why was I so specific?

"I see," says the policeman. He thinks for a moment. "It's a pity he's feeling that way, but it isn't uncommon. For some people, Harvest can be a very stressful time. Thanks for being willing to help him." Over all, the police don't seem particularly suspicious of my reason for being at the apartment and their questions don't continue for long. Finally, they turn to leave, and it can't happen quickly enough. But before they reach the living room door, the second policeman stops and asks to scan our Rice Grains and Ward Registration Cards, just as a precaution. I almost panic. What should I do? Object? Claim it's a violation of privacy? The police won't accept that; it will only make things worse. Suddenly I notice again the throbbing of the disruptive wrap. If Ken's technology is doing its job, the police scanners won't see my real ID, but what about the fake ID? Esther and I haven't managed to complete the first layer yet and I have no idea how much has been uploaded to my Rice Grain wrap in this first twenty-two minutes of the five thirty-minute processes. Maybe it'll be enough to fool some basic scanners, but a police scanner? Surely important chunks of the ID are still missing. But there's absolutely nothing I can do. I hand over my Ward Registration Card to be scanned; I know the Tamura ID is already firmly in place there. My hand is shaking but I disguise it by coughing.

"And your Rice Grain," the policeman soon says, handing back my card.

My throat feels tight; I want to throw up. I find myself subtly glancing around the room, trying to map an escape route: I'll be able to grab Esther's arm and pull her with me but I might have to hit one of the policemen with something hard to get by him. The other is holding the scanner so it'll take him a second or two to drop it and take out his stun gun. Maybe we'll get as far as the door, maybe not. *'This is impossible! We won't make it!'* I can't do it. My mind is screaming at me to act but not even desperation will give me enough adrenaline to move as fast as I'll need to. Once again, it's all going to come down to Ken's technology and the incomplete wrap. Very slowly, I turn away from the policeman to offer the back of my head, and as I do, I catch Esther's glance. She looks as terrified as I am. I close my eyes. *'Please let this work! Please!'*

"Thank you, Mr. Tamura," the policeman says. "And now your 'empty scan', if you don't mind. We have to check both Rice Grain locations in case of fraud; make sure you haven't got two Grains or two signatures. It's standard procedure, nothing to worry about." He walks round in front of me and scans my forehead to confirm there are no secondary Grain signatures, and then he turns to Esther. "And you, miss."

I can't turn around. Shock and relief in equal measure have temporarily stunned me. I can hardly believe it. Despite the process being less than one-fifth complete, the wrap is already able to fool a police scanner, one of the most powerful types of scanner around. I'm Michael Tamura in the eyes of the law, and the law is none the wiser. I sigh with relief, more audibly than I intend to, but no one seems to notice.

The police bow again. "Well, when you see Mr. Machida, please tell him that he should have gone to the Ward Office before leaving. And since this is also his birth ward, unless there are serious extenuating circumstances, he'll need to come back here to close his records before his Harvest. And another thing: tell him to keep his chin up and try to enjoy Harvest Day. Thanks for your time."

As soon as the police leave, I feel like an incredible pressure has been released from all around my body. The atmosphere has mercifully thinned and it's like I can move unimpeded again following some kind of sustained paralysis. I have no intention at all of going to the Ward Office so I don't spend much time thinking about it. Although returning to the ward of one's birth in order to close all personal records is something every Harvestee has to do, it's more of a formality rather than an actual law and so I'm happy to let it remain undone. There are more important things, although getting away from my apartment is no longer high on that list. The police have already found me, and they've already 'let me go' as it were. "This has been the second most stressful day of my life," I say to Esther, "But it really makes you appreciate it when things go well!"

Esther laughs, it seems more with relief than anything else. "You should have seen your face!"

"Don't joke!" I laugh back, also with relief. "I wanted to run! And you were just as bad!"

"Yeah, well." She knows I'm right. "Anyway, you've seen that the wrap works. I hope this means you're gonna be a bit more optimistic now."

I know I should be; I feel bad about still not being sure. What's wrong with me? Although I now have a new identity, my negativity remains unchanged, and I suddenly realise I've been somehow hoping there might be an infusion of Michael Tamura's fake confidence along with his fabricated history and counterfeit emotions. But there's nothing; this made-up man has left me to muster that part of the program myself. "That was a police scanner," I say, warily. "It wasn't the Harvest Light. Let's just finish all the layers first and get to the country, then I'll let you know how I feel."

I do notice one thing now, however: the warm throbbing sensation inside my head has stopped.

18
The Difference Between Nicholas Machida and Michael Tamura.

It's late so Esther spends the night at my place but neither of us are able to sleep particularly well. I'm plagued by fears of the coming Harvest, by doubts about the plan succeeding, but I'm also kept awake by my eager anticipation of soon being in the countryside. It's quite disconcerting to have such a contrast of emotions fighting for my attention. I feel almost like child again, wild with excitement waiting up for Christmas, only this time the penalty for being naughty isn't the withholding of presents but rather banishment to The Terror or death. Unfortunately, I think fear rather than excitement is winning the battle. Esther says she can't sleep because I can't sleep. That's empathy.

Rather than wasting valuable rest time, and as five hours have now elapsed since the police visit, we use another half an hour to apply the second layer of false ID to my Rice Grain wrap. This time, it goes much more smoothly with no interruptions. Esther even makes the procedure look easy, which I find reassuring.

We manage another hour or so of sleep after putting on the second Tamura layer but we still wake again early. It's like sleep deprivation is a side effect of the Rice Grain wrap, and it appears to be contagious to people aiding the process. Despite our growing exhaustion however, we decide there will be plenty of time to rest later and continue our preparations for departure. There are still a few hours before the 09:30 maglev so I cook a breakfast of rice and soup, making a mental note that this is my last ever breakfast in the city; I don't know why that matters. I also realise this is my second day without shaving and I've accumulated a messy but almost handsome stubble. For a few minutes, I wonder whether or not I should let it continue to grow: does Michael Tamura have a beard? But I soon realise he's just the same as me in that respect, totally undecided, so I shave it off.

After breakfast, Esther and I take the monorail back to her apartment for her to pack some things. Whilst she packs, I book us a couple of rooms at a cheap inn in the country, under the name Tamura. I've also packed clothes for myself, but as people taken by the Harvest are teleported with nothing other than what they're wearing at the time, I've only needed to pack for one night. It's a surprisingly unsettling feeling.

In spite of my being unsettled, this morning I think I really do feel a little more optimistic over all. I won't go so far as to say I'm feeling positive: there's no positive way to look at this nightmare, but I'm certainly less depressed than yesterday or the day before. The thought that we'll be in the country in a matter of hours and that I'll be fully 'wrapped' with the fictional Michael Tamura's ID give me a strange feeling that there's actually a chance, slight as it may be, that there can be a good resolution to all of this.

Soon we're on another monorail, this time headed for the train station, and I can't help but to stare out of the window and watch the city pass by. Now, although I really am certain it's the last time I'll see this view, I feel no sadness about it or any special connection. And there's certainly no desire to get out and walk. I hate the city. I hate what's happened to me here, what I've become because of it: once I was a reasonably happy and contented civil servant, and now I'm a terrified fugitive, hateful even of my own life. Perhaps what I told the police last night is actually true today: Nicholas Machida just can't bear to be here any longer.

By 09:10 we've bought our tickets and are stood on the maglev platform along with a multitude of happy Harvest Week holidaymakers, waiting for the army of cleaners to finish checking the carriages of the standing train. I'm reading and re-reading my ticket: *Tamura, Michael: car E, seat 21D.* I have to convince myself I'm Michael Tamura, not Nicholas Machida. There are so many unknown levels on which the Harvest Light works, I have to try and make this transformation as complete as possible: I have to truly believe I'm Michael Tamura in my mind and not just on my Rice Grain and Ward Registration Card. Maybe thinking this way will make a difference, maybe it won't, but I don't want to take any more chances than I already am. Once the final three layers of the Tamura ID are wrapped around my Grain, things will be better, I'm almost sure of it. Then I can try to forget about Nicholas Machida altogether.

I'm quietly impressed with myself when I very naturally respond to Esther calling me Michael and asking how long the journey is going to be. "Two and a half hours," I answer. "Then we've got a thirty-four minute wait until our next maglev. The second leg of the journey will only take an hour." I suddenly find myself brimming with tremendous pride at the fact that the people queuing behind me who probably overheard now believe my name's Michael. I don't know if I should really be feeling so happy at such a small and most likely inconsequential thing, but after a moment's consideration, I conclude that yes, I should. I might as well get some kind of enjoyment or satisfaction out of being Michael Tamura.

"Looks like the cleaners are finishing," says Esther. I can see them all standing in a line along the central aisle of the carriage closest to me. It looks like they're standing to attention, like they're listening to something, and after about thirty seconds, they bow, seemingly to no one in particular but still very co-ordinated, and file toward the exits. The train doors slide open and the eager passengers-to-be wait patiently for every last one of the cleaners to alight before boarding. Even children who'd previously been hounding their parents about when they might finally be able to get on board are standing still, thanking each cleaner as they pass. Such discipline never ceases to impress me.

The people queuing ahead of me step onto the train, and as they do so the door scanner reads their Rice Grains and an automated voice welcomes them onboard, each by name. I feel just a slight flutter in my stomach at first, but as I shuffle closer to the door, I also become aware that I'm feeling almost one hundred per cent confident that the train will believe I'm the man I'm pretending to be. After all, the people behind me believe I'm Michael Tamura, as do the police, and I'm sure that's a much bigger test of my Rice Grain wrap than a maglev train. As I step up, the female voice chirps, "Welcome, Tamura Michael", and for this very brief moment, I really do feel welcome.

Half an hour into the journey, I think I can finally say I'm feeling somewhat positive about things. Of course there's still a lot of uncertainty over whether or not the plan will actually work, but the closer we get to the country, the more I feel like I truly am heading toward refuge. It's a false refuge and I know that full well: the Harvest is tomorrow and there's no guarantee that being in the country will be any different to being in the city when the Harvest Light comes to read my false ID. Maybe it won't whisk me away although it's much more likely that it will, and if or when it does, I have no idea where it will take me. But until tomorrow, there's nothing I can do except carry out this, the only plan I have. Since last night, I've been mulling over Esther's and Minamoto's view that perhaps the Harvest might look mercifully on my 'mistake' if it somehow sees through my ID wrap. I'm still not particularly convinced about that but I find myself drawn to their optimism. What did Esther call it instead of optimism? *Hope.* I think that's something I've lacked in the past and it's only now that I'm starting to realise it. But whatever it's called, optimism or hope, it isn't easy to posses, though I think I'm learning. As the maglev blurs the city buildings, racing us toward our false refuge, I'm trying to make real the hope Esther has suggested, and for a time, the fact that the Harvest Light may be just as strong in the country as it is in the city, doesn't matter. Right now, amidst my mix of emotions, I almost feel free, or at least as though I've been granted a stay of execution, even if only for today. I guess maybe this is 'temporary hope'. It's a start.

I notice Esther is looking a little sombre so I ask her what's the matter. She doesn't reply immediately, it's clear she's struggling to find the correct words, but she eventually says, "I don't know. Is this right? Are we doing the right thing?"

My heart begins to pound. Esther's belief in the plan is the only reason I've gone through with it at all. Why, now that I'm beginning to have some confidence, is she beginning to doubt? "What do you mean, 'is this right'? You can't have second thoughts now!" I'm trying to keep my voice down. "This is serious! The Harvest is tomorrow! What happened to all of that hope? Are you thinking this isn't going to work now?" The back of my neck feels like it's tightening and I start to sweat.

"No, no, it could still work," Esther says, quietly. "Things may still be okay, I haven't changed my mind about that. I'm just concerned. I mean, well, we're trying to do the right thing, right? We're trying to prevent a bad thing from happening to you. But it seems we can't do that without breaking the law. It just doesn't make sense: breaking the law so that you don't go to The Terror. Isn't breaking the law what sends people there in the first place? I guess I'm just trying to understand the justice or the logic of it."

"Well don't," I say a little too abruptly, a sudden strength of conviction welling up inside me. "I'm way past thinking about justice and logic. I'm on to just hoping this all works. Anyway, you were all for this idea before. The thinking behind it didn't bother you. What on earth's changed?"

"Well, nothing really. I guess I'm just thinking a little bit about myself now too. We're both breaking the law, and we're not doing it by mistake. We're committing a crime."

"Try not to think about it like that. Yesterday when you called Ken, we only thought about it as a good and potentially life-saving idea, not as committing another crime. That hasn't changed, so try to focus on that."

"But I could be condemning myself by doing this."

I can't believe I've forgotten about this possibility; it's a horrific thought, even more terrible than my own condemnation. I'd rather go through with suicide or skip this whole plan and go straight to The Terror myself rather than have Esther be condemned. The idea of it gives me a sick feeling in my throat. But I know this isn't what she wants or needs to hear right now. I hold her arm. "Where's all this negativity coming from all of a sudden? I've picked up so much about optimism and hope from you. Are you just testing me now?" I smile, and I can see the corner of her mouth turn up a little. "You know what I've been thinking?" I continue, "I've been thinking about people like your friend Ken, and Kato, the salesman I met at the coffee shop. I was wondering why they go ahead and defy laws or try to bend the rules of the Harvest even though they know their own Harvest is inevitable. I was wondering why they bother, why they take such ridiculous risks. And I was also thinking about the things I've done in the past, and the things every person I've ever known has done, knowing full well that one day our Harvest'll come. And you know what? Even though we know we're not going to be in this city for ever, even though we know we're not supposed to do wrong if we want a good outcome at Harvest time, we can't help but push things to see what we can get away with. It doesn't make any sense but I think it's just the way we are. Okay, so we don't all commit serious crimes, but we've all got that element of rebellion in us. It's just natural for us so don't start thinking you're condemning yourself. You're just being human."

Esther turns to me. "I don't think you could say it's just 'natural' that I helped you get a false ID to avoid going to The Terror at Harvest. That's most definitely deliberate."

"I hear what you're saying, but you need to put things into perspective." I lean in closer and whisper into her ear, "You're not killing anyone. You're helping me do something you think is right. That's not a bad thing. Last night, you said you hoped the Harvest would be merciful. Now's the time to really hang on to that hope. If the Harvest is really so clever, it'll know you were doing what you felt was right when the time comes for you to go."

Esther breaks into a small smile. "Thanks," she says, softly. "You're a good friend. And you could be right. I still have a lot of hope, but you know the Harvest doesn't think the same way we do. There's much more to this system than we'll ever understand."

"Yeah, well maybe it should think the same way we do," I reply. "Then maybe we'd have a chance of understanding it."

There isn't a lot more conversation for the remainder of this leg of the journey. Esther falls asleep for a short time, but I can't. The anxiety I don't want to put on display to her is keeping me wide-awake. Keeping things from Esther isn't something I'm used to, but she looked so fragile telling me about her worries and the last thing I want to do is add to them. When we were growing up, it was always Esther encouraging me and spurring me on but now, so suddenly, things are reversed and here I am as the proverbial shoulder to cry on. So maybe not everything that's happened to me over the past couple of days has been negative after all: maybe as of this morning I've become a little more adept at seeking out positive traces in overwhelmingly negative situations. Just in time, it would seem. Perhaps this is my small subconscious contribution to the Michael Tamura persona. If so, given time, I think I could grow to like him.

19

Old Friends Come and Go, Particularly The Ones Who Aren't Friends.

We disembark in a large and surprisingly modern station boasting a stunning view of far-off tree-covered mountains and, beyond them, larger, rockier mounds, faint in the distance, rising ghost-like from the haze on the horizon. Although I can't be certain because it's quite hard to see, there may even be snow toward the top of some of the further rocky peaks. Low-level old-fashioned houses adorned with intricately tiled sloping roofs stretch away, further and further, until my eyes can no longer separate them and they become one long shimmering blur at the foot of the mountain range. This isn't quite the countryside yet: the buildings are still too densely packed together, the station still as crowded as any of the major hubs we've left behind, but there's already a certain clarity to the air and a sense of being removed from the all-consuming claustrophobia of the city. It makes Esther and I smile. "Y'know, I should have come out here more often," Esther realises, and I have to agree.

We squeeze past the other Harvest Week travellers down to the main mall of the station to look for somewhere to wait. "Okay, we've got half an hour before our next train. Do you want to get some lunch?" I ask.

"I'm not that hungry," Esther replies, "but I will have a snack. First I need the toilet. How about I meet you over at *Asa-Hiru.*" She points to the small café across the way from us where there are still a couple of empty seats, and she heads off to the ladies' washroom.

Sitting in the café, I try not to dwell too much on whether the plan will succeed or fail. The consequences of failure are more than I'll be able to handle, so I think it's better not to think about it at all, if that's possible. I find myself staring at the preoccupied commuters again like the afternoon I decided to commit suicide, and I start to ponder the liveliness of the station. For somewhere so far from the centre of the city, I'm surprised to find it so crowded, but I suppose with it being Harvest Week, now is the nationally acceptable time for most people to set aside their work responsibilities and travel. Even the DBDM will be closed tomorrow. As I watch the crowds surge and ebb and swell like the ocean I've seen countless times in movies, I wonder how many of these people are trying to escape the Harvest with false IDs. Very few if any, I imagine, bearing in mind the amount of money I've paid for the privilege. And besides, Rice Grain wrapping certainly isn't a common thing, so Ken tells me: it's more the reserve of the rich and powerful, or people of the criminal underworld, or the truly desperate. Still, anybody else attempting to do this probably hasn't left it until the last possible moment like I have. *'And why would they? Why would anyone who's broken the law want to try such a desperate thing as this?'* I ask myself. *'If they broke the law, surely admitting guilt and paying back the victim in the here and now would take away the need to try and escape Harvest? Well, that's if what Esther and Minamoto believe about the Harvest is true. But admitting to killing Nishi isn't going to bring him back or clear me. How can anyone atone for a killing? I've got no choice.'* Involuntarily, I'm back to thinking about my crime and punishment. "Think about something else!" I accidentally say out loud, and one of the other customers looks across at me. I look down and pretend I was reading from the menu. *'Hurry up, Esther, I'm going crazy sitting here on my own.'*

After ten minutes, Esther hasn't come back and I start to get concerned. She knows where to meet me and she also knows we only have twenty minutes remaining before our train departs. Still, she could have a perfectly good reason for being late.

After twenty minutes, I start to panic. I call her phone a few times but each time it fails to connect. I even go and stand outside the ladies' washroom and ask a couple of women leaving if they've seen a woman matching Esther's description still in there, but they haven't. Finally I go to the information desk and request a commuter announcement for Esther to meet me here at the desk or to call me immediately. The announcement is given straight away and twice more afterwards but there's no response. Five minutes remain until our train is scheduled to depart. I give the information desk staff my number and tell them to call me immediately if Esther shows up. Four minutes and thirty seconds. My chest is tightening, my stomach is turning and I don't know what to do. I'm becoming frantic. I run through the station, no idea where I'm going, trying to look into the face of every short-haired young woman who walks by just in case it's Esther, but they're all strangers. I push through the crowds, soon forgetting to apologise and bow, and all of the faces look at me, cold and disapproving, not caring at all that I'm in desperate trouble and have somehow lost the only woman who can help me. I want to run into the centre of the station and scream Esther's name, but the ounce of sanity I'm just managing to cling onto tells me this will be pointless. At two minutes to go before our train departs, I try phoning her again, without success, and return to the information desk for an update, but Esther still hasn't been seen. One minute. I charge up to the platform and board the train, scouring the car in which we've reserved seats, but there's no sign of her. "Esther, where are you!" I shout. I don't care what the other passengers think; I need to find her. But there's no reply. What should I do? Should I stay on board and head to the country? Perhaps Esther's somewhere else on the train and she'll appear once we're under way. But maybe she isn't onboard at all, maybe she's still somewhere in the station. There isn't the time I need to think this through properly, but I can't go without her. I leap back onto the platform just as the train doors begin to close. "This isn't happening!" I cry out. "Esther!"

I turn to watch the train slowly levitate off the track and begin it's gentle glide out of the station, and for just a moment, I don't know which feels worse: being left behind by the train and seeing my chances of escape diminish, or the fact that Esther has suddenly gone missing. But it's Esther my mind dwells on: she's more important than my getting to the country. I feel scared for her. Something terrible must have happened for her not to return, but what? There have been no alarms, no reports of accidents anywhere in the station, absolutely nothing that seems out of the ordinary. I'm completely helpless once again, but now that my fears aren't just about my own situation but also about the safety of the only friend I have in this nightmare world, this new powerlessness is far worse than before.

I spend the next two and a half hours wandering around the station, every few minutes calling Esther's phone and checking at the information desk, but she doesn't appear. I even duck into the ladies' washroom, something I should have done sooner, but she isn't there. Thankfully, however, neither is anyone else, though if there were, I honestly don't think I'd care too much. Eventually, I build up the courage to go to the station security office. I know I should also have done this sooner, but I've been wanting to avoid contact with the authorities as much as possible; I'm trying not to forget that I'm a fugitive. But I have to do something.

Taking a picture of Esther from me, the security staff try matching it and a description of her clothing with footage from the station cameras. They manage to spot someone who could be Esther entering the ladies' washroom just at the time she and I separated but they're unable to identify anyone similar leaving the washroom after that. And now they're asking me if I want to contact the police. It would have been easier if they hadn't given me a choice. The agony of the decision is almost too much for me to bear: can I risk letting slip my real identity in a traumatised babble and throw away any last chance of escape by bringing the police in, or should I leave them out of it and hope Esther will turn up? Surely there's no real decision here? Surely Esther is my main priority? But it takes some very serious deliberation before I finally decide to call the police, and I'm more than shocked and disappointed with myself; I'm completely devastated. '*What the hell's the matter with me?*' is all I can think. I'm the very lowest of all human beings. *'Maybe I don't deserve to escape.'*

It doesn't take long for the police to arrive, so I don't have much time to try and calm down. It isn't so much the thought of speaking to them now that's bothering me, but rather that I honestly considered putting myself before my friend like that. I had no idea I could be so selfish, so despicable, and this brief glimpse into my deeper character makes me extremely angry. I want to punish myself by confessing everything to them and I almost do, but I find a faint trace of Nicholas Machida's indecision and hesitation somehow holding me back. *'Should I* this*? Will it* that*? Blah blah blah.'* I want to tell him to shut up but the police are already talking to me.

Actually, my encounter with the police isn't so difficult. They only question me briefly about my connection to Esther, what our recent histories are (obviously, mine is completely made up), and where Esther and I had been heading to this afternoon. They take down her description and what she had with her, and I make a special effort to omit the fact that she was carrying Rice Grain wrapping equipment, which is also now missing. They scan my Rice Grain and Ward Registration Card, and it's at this point that I feel near indescribable relief that despite hardly caring at all now about my fake ID, I've still given my name as Michael Tamura. I don't want to think about what would have happened had I confessed to my real identity at the start of the interview. After explaining all I can to the police, they tell me they're going to carry out a thorough search of the station and put out an alert for Esther, but there's nothing more I can do right now and they suggest I return to the city. I want to stay at the station and I tell them exactly that, but they insist I go, and it's rarely a good idea to argue with the police, even when not wearing an illegal Rice Grain wrap.

I have to wait almost two hours for a maglev heading back to the centre of the city and I spend the entire time searching for Esther and calling her phone, all without success. I've spent over five hours at the train station and every minute of it, aside from perhaps the first ten, has been awful. When the train eventually does arrive, the two and a half hour journey back seems to take forever. I speak to no one for the whole journey and I can't even remember the train's automated voice welcoming me onboard. *'But why should it?'* I ponder. *'I don't deserve goodwill from anyone, not even from a machine.'* This extra time to think isn't very productive. Other than resolving to tell Ken what's happened in the faint hope that he might be able to help in some way, I can only replay the train station events in my mind, wondering if there was any hint from Esther that she intended not to come back. True, she was quite worried before we arrived at the station, but I know Esther: nothing she said or did suggested she was going to run away. Something happened to her, I'm almost sure of it. "Where are you?" I whisper.

I'm alone and hopeless again, and now, almost as though the thought of suicide has been lying dormant, waiting patiently for the perfect conditions to return, it suddenly pops back into my mind. Now that my only reason for not having gone through with it in the first place has vanished, surely there's no point in putting myself through further anguish? Except I can't leave things like this. I have to know what's happened to her. Although there's no guarantee I'll ever find out, I can't throw away any chance of knowing by killing myself. I have to hold on. Until my Harvest in less than twenty-four hours, I'll wait for the police, I'll keep calling Esther's phone, and if the stress becomes too much, maybe I'll get very drunk.

20
The Right Number.

Riding the high-speed train back into the centre of the city feels like being injected into a huge torture machine designed to maim and kill with efficiency and variety. As soon as I step down onto the platform, I'm assaulted by the aggressive humidity, and the darkness I can see outside only adds to my sense of being smothered by something vast yet somehow intangible. But I feel that even before the very air itself will manage to suffocate me, I'm going to be battered mercilessly by the grotesquely swollen crowds of commuters and chewed up by the gauntlet of security gates and leisure machines even before I make it to the exit. It's almost a genuine surprise to see that I'm still alive a few minutes later, waiting for a taxi to Ken's apartment.

The insurance claims investigator is surprised to see me, but I waste no time with pleasantries and Ken's surprise quickly turns to horror when I tell him what's happened. Twice, he asks me to explain in minute detail all of the events at the station and, as much as I can remember, everything Esther and I said to each other on the train. I can tell Ken's impressive mind is already picking apart every bit of information while I speak, trying to analyse it from alternative angles, hopefully gleaning clues and ideas that I've missed. He even produces a palm-sized screen from his pocket and starts tapping information into it. But despite this giving me some slight hope for just a little longer than it takes me to explain everything, the look of worry and defeat on his face once I've finished soon snatches that hope away again.

"And the police said nothing else?" he asks once more.

"No, nothing. It's ridiculous. They only promised to keep looking and put out alerts. Anything could have happened to her. Don't you know some way of searching for her Rice Grain or checking if it's been scanned anywhere?"

"Following a trail of Rice Grain scans is possible but only by precinct-based police computers tied directly into the Security Network. I don't have access to a precinct-based police computer or anything that emulates one, plus there are only a handful of them and they're monitored all the time. Trust me, if there was any way I could do that, I would. But the police will have done that already anyway."

"Why can't we just pinpoint her Rice Grain?" I cry. "Why don't we have a satellite system for that?"

"Now we're moving into politics," says Ken. "You tell me why they never vote to have one."

'You're part of the criminal world! You tell me!' I suddenly feel quite ashamed to have thought this about Ken and I'm glad I didn't say it out loud. "So what the hell am I supposed to do?" I say instead. "Doesn't any of this stuff you've got lying around help?"

"Not for finding people who vanish into thin air. The Rice Grain wrapping equipment's tagged so I should've been able to find that, but the trace I just tried drew a total blank. That shouldn't happen." He shows me the screen he's been holding and it's blank but for the line *'EQUIPMENT F29CA2B NOT FOUND'* flashing in the corner. "That really shouldn't happen at all," he says again. "Can't you go back to the police?"

"What good will that do?" I stop and think for a moment. Ken may actually be right. Although I don't feel the police are helping much at all, I'm not going to get any miracle techno-solutions from Ken. He hasn't even been able to trace his equipment. Exactly what else the police might be able to do, I have no idea, but anything has to be better than just waiting.

Reluctantly, I decide to go to the nearest police station and get up to leave, but as I pick up my phone, it chimes, signalling that I've received a non-audio message. Both Ken and I anxiously catch our breath. We're hoping it's Esther, but it could be the police. As I see the display, I don't recognise the originating phone number, and when I open the message, I suddenly don't know what to feel at all. It reads, *'SHE'S OKAY.'*

"Who's it from?" Ken asks.

"I don't know!" I reply, irritated, and scroll back to the phone number. I try calling it but there's no response other than an automated voice stating that the number I've tried to call is invalid. Frustrated, I try again with the same result.

"Try sending a non-audio back," Ken suggests.

"It just said the number's invalid."

"Yet you still just got a message from that number. Just try it!"

He's right, I might as well try. I return to the message, hit 'reply', and dictate, "Who are you? Where's Esther?" The words stream across the display, *'WHO ARE YOU? WHERE'S ESTHER?'* and as I send the message, I plead, "Please don't say it's invalid! Please!"

We wait in agonising silence for what feels like hours, though it's really only about thirty seconds, and the phone chimes again. *'MEET ME AT THE COFFEE SHOP OF THE KETTEI BUILDING RIGHT NOW. IT WOULD BE BETTER NOT TO INVOLVE THE POLICE.'*

I gasp. "What? The coffee shop of the Kettei Building?"

Ken frowns. "Is that significant?"

"It's the same coffee shop where I met Kato the salesman the day before yesterday, and Minamoto from the office yesterday afternoon." Is this a coincidence? Surely not? I pull out the two men's business cards and compare the numbers but neither of them match the number on my phone. Still, if it really is one of them, they could be using another phone to message me. I notice Ken's frown deepening, his face contorting as though he's having trouble processing a train of thought and it's causing him pain. It even starts to worry me. "What's the matter?" I ask, hoping he's figuring out something useful and not about to collapse.

"Hang on a second," he says and takes the phone from me. He's now mouthing sequences of numbers, stopping every few seconds to look confused before resuming sequences. After a mini conversation with himself, much of it in his mind apparently, though I do catch a few words about numbers and satellites, he hands the phone back. "This phone number isn't right," he says to me at last. "Look at the opening arrangement: it isn't a carrier code – not of any kind. It's, well, it's gobbledegook. It doesn't mean anything. It doesn't make any sense."

I can't pretend to know what he's talking about. To me, it's just another phone number. And suddenly it's like a dormant part of my mind switches on. "Wait a minute. I think I *have* seen this number before." I push the number up to the top corner of my display and start searching through the phone history to compare it. Somehow, now that my attention's been drawn to the strange arrangement, I'm almost certain I've seen this number recently, but just not thought anything of it at the time. And now I find it. I received a call from this number three days ago. But I can't remember speaking to Kato, Minamoto, or any strangers on the phone three days back, only to Esther herself. But now I see the time: the call had been at 13:14, the exact moment I was to step out in front of the train. And the caller had been a man claiming to have dialled the wrong number, looking for a Mr. Nishi.

21
Good Night.

Ten minutes after receiving the anonymous message, I'm in a taxi on my way to the Kettei building coffee shop, and it suddenly strikes me how much trust I'm putting in what I've been told. How do I know Esther's really okay? Why shouldn't I call the police? I have no idea who sent the message or why, or even how for that matter: the phone number doesn't appear to be valid – except for when it wants to be; I could be racing headlong into further trouble for all I know. But there's no other action I can take: I have to make sure Esther's alright and that's all there is to it. She is the most important thing to me now.

Despite the advice not to get the police involved – which curiously does come across more as advice than instruction, and I re-read it over and over again to be certain – I still want to call them. Esther's in danger, I'm sure of it: in danger from whom, I don't yet know, but I do know it's more than Ken or I are able to handle. Even with Ken's dealings with people on the wrong side of the law, he tells me he's neither experienced nor equipped to go up against kidnappers (or whatever these people are) and I have no trouble believing him. Whoever these people may be, they clearly have tremendous resources. It's evident they've been watching me closely for a number of days now; how else would they have known about my suicide bid, my association with Esther, my attempt to escape? A thought that should have been obvious now occurs to me: *'They know about my crime!'* I suddenly feel vulnerable and exposed again, the same disorientating fear I felt when I went to withdraw cash from the open-air Teller Point. How many people know what I've done? I see the taxi driver glance at me in his mirror: there's something about his expression; does he know too? Reason suggests not and I close my eyes to stop the spinning sensation I can feel beginning. I take deep breaths and try to steady myself on the seat until the dizzying movement in my head stops but it does nothing to take away my intense sense of defeat. It seems like all of my attempts to hide over the past few days have been utterly futile, like someone has been following me around, spying on me the whole time. I realise now that in my mind I'd successfully been distancing myself from my guilt, I'd been gradually growing in hope and optimism as the plan progressed, and now I'm suddenly right back where I started three days ago. I feel as bloodied as the morning I pulled the trigger.

What do they want with me? Blackmail? Then why kidnap Esther? Why not just threaten to expose me? I'd have no hesitation in paying whatever money I have left to keep my crime from getting out. Why all of this trouble? Why follow me? I may well be a fugitive but I obviously still have far to go before I properly understand the criminal mind.

If I'm somehow being monitored, it seems clear these people will know immediately if Ken or I contact the police. It's just not worth the risk and I don't even want to speculate on the consequences if that happens. Instead, we've formed a very rough plan, or rather Ken has. He's following some distance behind in another taxi and with any luck, he'll be able to video the meeting from a hidden vantage point using some rather impressive long-range equipment, after which he'll attempt to follow the contact person. We can't risk me following the contact after the meeting concludes in case this group has another person following me from a distance. It's very messy and far from perfect, but it's all we can do right now, and before I feel like I've had any time to prepare myself, my taxi lands in front of the coffee shop.

It's after 21:00 but the shop is still fairly busy. From the door, I search the customers' faces for anyone I recognise or for anyone signalling me to approach, but everyone looks engrossed in conversation or in a book or in their own thoughts. They all look distinctly unburdened and I envy them. What do I do now? How do I subtly ask every customer here if they've been involved in a kidnapping this afternoon? And suddenly I see at the same table where I met Kato on the day I tried to kill myself, the fifty-three year old bet-hedging salesman is sat, drinking his coffee. My fists clench and my ears feel like they've burst into flames. I've never felt so much rage directed at one person in my entire life and I stride toward him, not yet sure what I'm going to do, though it will probably start with punching him in the face. Kato doesn't even seem to notice me approach, but as I get to the table, I realise that angering the kidnapper isn't the best start. I stand straight in front of him and growl in a low voice so as not to draw too much attention, "Where is she? Why did you take her?"

Kato looks up and he seems a little startled. "Mr. Machida? What are you doing here?"

"What do you mean, 'what am I doing here?' I got your message. What have you done with Esther?"

Kato looks genuinely confused and I start to feel awkward, like I may have made a terrible mistake. "You got my message?" he repeats. "I haven't sent you any messages. What are you talking about?"

Now I'm worried. "What?"

A look of simultaneous realisation and disappointment suddenly draws across Kato's face. "Oh, right. I should've guessed."

I now notice the salesman is no longer looking at me but past me and I turn to see Minamoto standing behind me.

"You?" I gasp.

"Me," Minamoto says quietly. "But it's really not what you think." He sits down beside Kato.

"Can't you sit somewhere else?" Kato says, looking very annoyed.

Minamoto doesn't seem to care. "Sorry, busy night, no free tables." There are plenty of free tables. "Machida, why don't you sit down," he says, and nudges an empty chair toward me.

"You two know each other?" I hiss.

Neither man says anything but Minamoto tilts his head slightly. I don't know if this means yes or no. He indicates the seat again and I sit down, very confused.

"Isn't this interesting, the three of us sitting here?" Minamoto smiles. His tone is almost playful.

Kato sips his coffee but doesn't look up. "Yeah, isn't it just."

My anger and confusion and their apparent calm are an unstable combination and I almost bang on the table in frustration. "What the hell's going on?" I whisper, sharply. "Where's Esther?"

Kato the salesman ignores me and turns to Minamoto. "I hear he got a message to meet me here. Isn't that against some law or something?"

"Actually," Minamoto replies, "he got a message to meet *me* here. And I hear his closest friend just disappeared. Isn't that against some law?"

Kato turns to me. "I don't expect you to see the bigger picture, Mr. Machida, but this is just a means to an end."

"You took her?" I want to grab him. "What have you done to her? Where is she?"

"I can't tell you that. And neither can he." The salesman indicates Minamoto. "But she's perfectly safe. As I said, it's just a means to an end."

I can't follow what's going on. "Is this all about you escaping Harvest? How the hell does kidnapping Esther help you do that?" And as I'm speaking, I suddenly realise what he must be doing. "You want the false ID. Is it just about that? Well I don't care about it, you can have it. Just give me back Esther!"

"Don't try to figure things out, Mr. Machida," says Kato. "I don't need your false ID. And besides, surely there's no way I could've known before that you were planning to escape using a Rice Grain wrap, right?" He finishes his coffee. "You'll get Esther back tomorrow. In the meantime, I suggest you get some rest. It's gonna be a big day!" He stands up to leave. "Oh, just in case you no longer think I'm a man of my word, what I said yesterday still stands. If you're still looking for a way out, I'll leave a storage cylinder here tomorrow morning with your name on it. Well, with one of your names on it. Let's say 'Michael Tamura'." He smiles, returns his cup to the counter and leaves without another word.

I'm almost numb with disbelief; it's this that stops me from following him out. How could he possibly have known the plan? He even knew my false name. Did he interrogate Esther to get this information? If he's hurt her, I don't know what I'll do. But I can't end the meeting here. Shakily, I stand up to follow but Minamoto holds on to me. "I wouldn't bother trying to follow him. Seriously, trust me," he says.

I pull free and run as best as I can out of the coffee shop but Kato is already gone. As my wits and balance return, I race up the street and back down again past the shop entrance, I search round the corners of the massive office building and even scan the underground car park, but there's no sign of him. But all may not be lost. Hopefully Ken is following him so I return inside to Minamoto. "And why should I trust you?" I ask before he has the chance to say anything. "Are you working with him?"

"Of course I'm not," Minamoto says, as though it's ridiculous for me to think so. "I sent you the messages."

"Why did you do that if you're not going to tell me where she is? You obviously know. If you really want to be helpful, bring her back!"

"It doesn't work like that."

"What doesn't work like that? It's easy. You obviously have a lot of resources so use them!" It's hard for me not to shout, although the other customers already know something unpleasant is going on. "And who are you anyway?" I seethe. There are so many things I need to know. I remember the phone number that isn't a phone number. "Did you call me at the train station three days ago?"

"Yes."

"How did you know I was there? Did you know what I was going to do?"

"You've got a lot of questions but –."

"You're damned right I've got a lot of questions. So give me some answers. Who are you?"

"Right now, that's not important," says Minamoto. He's also trying to keep his voice low. "The reason I sent you the message is so that you know Esther's okay. You've got enough to deal with already and it wasn't fair for him to take her."

"Wasn't fair? Are you people playing a game or something? What are you, gangsters? Secret Service? How are you able to do all of this?"

Minamoto dodges the question. "Look, Kato was right, tomorrow's going to be a big day, so you need to get some rest. I just wanted you to know Esther's okay so that you can concentrate on what you need to do about your Harvest."

"I don't care about my Harvest!" I also don't care that I've shouted this and startled some of the customers.

Minamoto suddenly looks very serious. "Don't lose focus, Machida. Everything's about Harvest. Now you should go home." He stands up to leave but this time I hold on to him.

"I don't understand," I sigh, loudly, "I really don't. There's obviously something going on here that I'm missing. So if you're trying to help me, you need to give me more than this."

Minamoto looks at me with what seems to be compassion. I'm in such a state however, I could well be misinterpreting his face: it could be regret I'm seeing. Either way, it appears he wants to say more than he's allowing himself to. "Seriously, the best thing you can do right now is rest. You're under a lot of stress and tomorrow is Harvest Day. Go home, take some natural camomile and go to bed. Really." He bows and leaves but I don't try to follow him.

I hoped to get some answers from this meeting but instead I'm now more confused than before. And matters aren't helped when Ken walks in a couple of minutes after Minamoto leaves.

"What are you doing here?" I ask him. "Did you follow Kato?"

"No," says Ken, angrily. "There was no point. He knew I was there."

"What? How did he know?"

"No idea. I was completely hidden, but when he left, he looked straight in my direction and waved."

This is nearly too much for me to take. "Well what about Minamoto?" I ask. "Couldn't you have tried following him?"

"Minamoto?" Ken says. "He didn't wave, he just smiled at the camera and said, 'Goodnight, Mr. Ida'. Who the hell are those two?"

I don't know how to answer him.

I return home incensed, drained and emotionally worn out, but I'm unable to sleep. It's not that I can't sleep; it's that I don't want to. The thought of following Kato and Minamoto's advice to get some rest – or to do anything at all that they suggest – makes me furious. They seem to be playing a stupid game with my life, and with Esther's life, but to what end? And to add to my frustration, they've clearly demonstrated that there's absolutely nothing I can do about it. I still have no idea who they really are, but I'm fairly certain Tristan Kato isn't a salesman, Simon Minamoto probably doesn't really work for the DBDM, and I'm way out of my depth. Despite Minamoto's assurance that Esther is safe and Kato's promise to return her tomorrow, I'm still worried for her safety. What do they want with her? How is kidnapping her related to my Harvest? For the rest of the night and into the early morning, I watch the clock counting down the remaining hours of my life here and I agonise over questions I have no chance of figuring out the answers to. How is it that each terrible night has somehow managed to beat the previous terrible night in just how bad things can get? Surely this is more than a person can or should have to bear.

Eventually, I concede that I'm wasting my time and energy in this stubborn effort not to follow the advice of the two men in the coffee shop, and I crawl, utterly exhausted, onto my bed. As fatigue pulls me to sleep, I realise I haven't had any camomile as Minamoto suggested, and now I wonder if this constitutes a small victory. It's the only good thing about tonight.

22

The Sacrifice of Cake for Something Less Lethal.

I thought I'd got away with not having to give a farewell speech to my work colleagues but somehow, here I am sitting at my desk, and everyone is standing around me, expectantly. I stand up. I know I've already been speaking, I know I've said a lot to them already, but I can't remember what any of it was, and I feel nervous. For some reason, I think there's a chance I might have accidentally confessed to everyone that I shot and killed a man on my way to work this morning. The fact that everyone seems present and accounted for suggests that no one has ducked out to call the police so it's possible the confession was just in my head. Still, I can't shake off this uneasy feeling that I've already said more than I should have.

"Mr. Machida?" my department head whispers, trying to prompt me to continue.

"Ah, sorry sir," I stammer, snapping out of my haze. "Oh, and I think you have to call me Tamura now. I'm not Machida anymore."

"Of course, my apologies, Mr. Tamura," my department head politely smiles. "You were saying?"

I have no idea what I was saying. "Erm, I'd like to thank everyone for coming to say goodbye. Have I already said this?"

My department head nods.

"Okay. Well, erm, I guess it's been a privilege to work here and I've really appreciated everyone's professional attitude. I'll miss you all." I see Minamoto standing at the back of the gathering of well-wishers. "Except you, Minamoto. I hate you so I'm not going to miss your stupid face at all. Or yours, Kato." Kato has just appeared beside him. "In fact…" I growl and run through the crowd who seem to have increased two-fold. As I get to Kato, I throw my fist at his face with all of my strength and it connects well but the impact hardly shakes him.

"Yeah, I'll miss you too, Nick or Michael or whatever your name is," he says, rubbing his cheek. "You're lucky I'm not fighting back."

My department head places himself between us but there's no need. I feel exhausted after just the one punch and I have no intention of fighting anymore. "Come on, you two. There's no need to leave on such a bad note, Mr. Tamura. Ah look, your driver's here." He indicates toward the door.

The chauffeur with the large bushy beard is waiting for me and I instantly feel depressed. "Oh don't be like that, Mr. Tamura," the chauffeur says. "Where do you want to go?"

I don't want to answer him but I eventually say, "We've had this conversation before. Aren't you taking me to The Terror?"

"Eventually. Maybe," the chauffeur says. "But where do you want to go first?"

"Look, I really don't care!" I snap. "Just take me wherever you want!"

The chauffeur smiles, though it's difficult to see this through his beard. "I know just the place!"

I don't remember the taxi ride. One moment I was at the office, talking to the chauffeur, and now I'm standing alone on the shore of a silent lake. I've been here before, there was an eagle and a fish with me, but now I have no idea where they are. This must be part of the countryside; there are no buildings anywhere, only the gravel shore and green hills bordering this huge stretch of water, and the sky looking larger and emptier than I've ever seen it before. It seems so close I feel I might be able to touch the gathering clouds if I really try. I trace an invisible line down to the horizon where the enormous lake intersects with the expanse of the sky and I see a brilliant glow that appears to be drawing closer at quite a speed. Soon I see that the whole surface of the lake is somehow ablaze, but before I become too frightened, I remember that the eagle has gone hunting for cakes and that the last time I was here, it was a dream. I hope this is a dream too and that I wake up soon because the fire is getting very close now.

23
Background Noise.

Even before I open my eyes, I can see the bright glow through my weighted eyelids. The flames must be all around me now but I don't feel like I'm burning. I don't even feel hot. At first I find this surprising and it makes we wonder why I've always been so scared of fire if it doesn't actually hurt, but I soon remember that the burning lake was just a dream and I'm in the process of waking up. I can feel my pillow under my head and the gentle cushioning of my mattress, but the glow is still here. Why is there still a glow around me?

'The Harvest Light!'

My eyes shoot open in absolute horror and I leap off the bed, rolling to the door to try and escape from it, but I already know escape is impossible. It's too late. Everything is bathed in amber: it's the most terrifying thing I've ever seen. *'Please, not yet!'* I don't know if I've shouted this only in my mind or out loud.

It takes me a few seconds to realise that this isn't the Harvest Light at all; it's sunlight altered slightly by my beige curtains to resemble the thing I perhaps fear most in the entire world, and I feel like a complete idiot. Despite the fact that nearly every summer morning for over five years, I've woken up to this very same yellow-orange tinted sight and not thought a thing about it, today it seems to have taken on a whole new amber menace. I already suspect that everything I see and do today will in some way reflect this oncoming doom. But more than my feelings of underlying despair and idiocy, I feel relieved: I'm safe, for the moment. But only for the moment. I start to breathe again, only now realising that I've been holding my breath since gasping at the sight of amber light flooding my bedroom, and my heart rate slowly returns to something resembling normal, but I'm still frightened. It's late, 09:23; I've got just a few hours at most before the Harvest Light will be upon me for real. There won't be any mistaking *it* for sunlight.

I didn't intend to sleep so long and an annoyance with myself starts to kick in. What if Kato or Minamoto called with important information and I missed it? Then what? Come to think of it, I don't actually know if I'm just supposed wait for one of them to contact me at all or if I'm supposed to do something myself. They never said, and for some reason, I didn't think to ask. But I can't just sit around waiting. I grab my phone and try calling Esther. Like yesterday, there's no answer. Kato said he'd return her, but where to? Will he send her home? Will she turn up on my doorstep? Another question worries me; I don't want to ask it, but the threat is real: will she even be alive? I have no reason to believe that Kato and Minamoto are telling the truth about her being unharmed, or even that she'll be returned at all, but I'm completely at their mercy. I can't stand it. Whether they're working together or not, I hate them both. (I seem to remember telling them so but I can't think when it might have been. Surely I wouldn't have said it last night and risked angering them? It must have been a dream.) Despite how I feel, I have to speak to them and I try calling the two men on their business card numbers but there's no reply from either. I call the strange number Minamoto used to message me last night but again, I only get the automated invalid number response. Sending a dictated message this time also gets no reply, only an instant non-audio version of the same 'invalid number' message. It's like I've been cut off from the world. I try telephoning again: first Esther, now Kato, now Minamoto, now the message number: still nothing. I send another dictation. Nothing. I repeat all of this again. And again. I try Esther twice in a row, Kato twice in a row, Minamoto twice in a row, the message number twice in a row, in case doing that somehow makes a difference. It doesn't – of course it doesn't; why would I think it would? With every call and every message, I'm begging for someone to answer, soon I'm audibly pleading for anyone at all to respond, and I'm sure my next-door and upstairs neighbours can hear me pacing between my bedroom, my tiny lounge, my even tinier kitchen, occasionally shouting out loud for an answer, but I really don't care what they can hear. This is important – more important than what the people around me think. But it's like there's nobody out there; it's like all of the people I really need to speak to no longer exist. *'What the hell's going on?'* I'm sure I've shouted this out loud. I want to try phoning again but suddenly my body feels almost rigid, I feel that I shouldn't call, that doing so and getting the same negative result will only make me feel even more alone, even more helpless than I already do. Maybe it's some kind of defence mechanism: perhaps my body knows something my brain doesn't about how much more pressure I can take.

I don't understand why any of this is happening; why I've killed a man, how I've become caught up in this whole nightmare, why Esther has been kidnapped, why I'm now completely isolated from everyone at the very time I need to know exactly what to do. I'm finding it hard to breathe and I open a window to get some fresh air, but the air that pours in is hot and thick, even more stifling than the air inside, so it doesn't help. I have to try calling again, I can't just sit idly. I resist the stiffness in my arm and the inexplicable urge to do nothing, and this time I try calling Kato first. As the number dials, I pray that he'll answer. I don't know who or what I'm praying to; maybe to my deceased ancestors again, maybe to something else, maybe even to Kato himself, and I almost retch when there's no connection. My throat feels tight and my gut like it's preparing to churn out the little I've eaten over the past twenty-four hours. I try Minamoto straight away, eyes closed, gritting my teeth, and when there's no connection there either, I curse and kick the sofa. I'm starting to feel dizzy again, it's become a recurring nausea, so I sit down. And as soon as I sit, from nowhere I'm attacked by a near overpowering sense of vulnerability, or paranoia, like some man-sized embodiment of the Harvest is about to leap into my apartment through the open window and grab me. I get up quickly, close the window, and sit down again before I fall over. Maybe I'm starting to lose my mind.

I struggle to send a new dictated message to Minamoto's mysterious message number but I get the same automatic response as before: *'SORRY, THE NUMBER YOU HAVE TRIED TO SEND A MESSAGE TO IS INVALID'*. I swear at the phone. I can feel myself getting heavier: it's like the gravity in the room is increasing and I'm being pulled to the floor. I can barely lift my rebelling body to sit upright. Almost lying across the sofa, my weak thumb touches Esther's name on the phone display and once again, it goes straight to her video messaging service. She's introducing herself with her usual enormous smile and telling her caller to say something nice otherwise she won't call back. It's almost like I'm seeing her face from beyond the grave. She looks so happy, so like the Esther I know. How different must she be looking right now, how terrified, that's if she's alive at all? I can't take any more of this recording, seeing her dear face but not knowing how or where she is;

it's just too much: I use the trace of energy I have left to hang up. A further increase in gravity now pulls my barely raised head down into the fabric of the sofa and the growing pressure inside the room squeezes at my temples until they're almost fit to burst. I can feel my face contorting, the muscles tightening involuntarily, my eyes bulging, but there are no tears: it's like I've already been emptied of everything. I can only lay here and stare. My mind deserts me too, I feel like a used-up, pointless shell. This is what it is to be truly defeated, to be completely and utterly without hope. There's nothing left now. The Harvest will be here soon.

I don't know how long I've been lying here. I don't think I've heard a single sound, I certainly haven't moved, I don't even recall blinking, but I'm fairly certain I've been here for a while. It feels like I've been in a void, starved of all of my senses, and now I'm emerging. My thumb is moving; it's dialling Esther again from the phone still in my hand. My eyes are only half focused on the display but suddenly I see Esther's face and hear her voice and I sit bolt upright. But it's her video message again. The anger that unexpectedly explodes from inside me is unnerving. I scream out loud and hurl the phone across the room. Luckily, it bounces off a chair and lands harmlessly on the floor. It isn't like me to have an outburst like this, but I'm sure there's very little of *me* left: the man I was before Harvest Week, the innocent civil servant looking forward to seeing his fiancé again, is long gone. For a second, I wonder if this transformation is more complete and effective than the unfinished Rice Grain wrap on my brainstem: in some way, the old Nicholas Machida really doesn't exist anymore. But I don't think the Harvest Light will be convinced. Actually, I'm not convinced either. However things look, whether to me or to the Harvest Light, I know I can't go on like this. I have no desire to go on at all. I wish I'd kept Nishi's gun and not thrown it back: one bullet could end this whole nightmare right now. Maybe I should try throwing myself under a train again.

Suddenly, I remember Kato's offer: if I'm still looking for a way out, he'll leave a storage cylinder for me at the coffee shop. I don't know why I remember this now; aside from death, I don't think I'm looking for another way out anymore. It's over for me; I can't chase vain hopes or put my trust in mysterious strangers any longer. There's just no point. But on the other hand, what do I have to lose? I'm not sure I can really believe Kato about the storage cylinder – I certainly know I can't trust him – but perhaps doing something, anything, is better than sitting here falling further and further into suicidal depression. Maybe Esther's hope has run deeper in me than I first thought.

As I pick up my phone to go out, I notice a low, continuous hum, barely audible. It's coming from outside. I realise it's been there for quite a while now, blending in to the ambient nothingness of my limbo, but somehow it hasn't registered properly with me until this moment: maybe I've been too lost in my despair to acknowledge it, perhaps I've been subconsciously blocking it out, but it's definitely there. It sounds very far away but there's no mistaking what it is. I race out of the door, forgetting even to put my shoes on, my heart pounding even more than when I woke in terror this morning, and I round the side of my building, hoping that somehow I'm wrong. But I'm not wrong. There to the east, stretching all across the horizon and endlessly up into the sky, the great Harvest Light has begun to make its pass through the city.

24
The Third.

I can't breathe. It's not even that I'm forgetting to this time. I'm trying but my lungs feel like they're made of stone, my windpipe like it's not even there. In panic, I punch myself hard in the chest to kick-start my breathing, and it thankfully works before I become too starved of oxygen to stay conscious. This is the fifth Harvest I've seen, but if a person were to see even a thousand Harvests, each time would be like the first time all over again: unbelievable, astounding, terrifying. The third important thing suddenly comes to mind: although the process of the Harvest may appear frightening, it really shouldn't be feared, provided we haven't done wrong. I have plenty of reason to be frightened.

The awesome sight of this vast moving wall of amber light is almost too much to take in. Even with it here before me, the sheer size of it is simply incomprehensible; it's so huge it has no visible edge, it's like the amber sky has been turned on its side and set in motion toward me; like I'm slowly falling toward an endless sea of molten lava. I can't stare at it too long for fear of being driven mad by the sheer magnitude of this phenomenon. But today it's worse: today, this staggering, overwhelming sight is coming for me. At a terrified guess, it's only about 10 kilometres away. If I'm to do anything now, I have to hurry.

Riding on the monorail, I'm all too aware that going to the Kettei Building coffee shop to retrieve Kato's storage cylinder means heading toward the Harvest Light. If my estimate is right, I still have around one and a half hours before it reaches me, but it isn't enough time. Witnessing the Light directly seems to have disintegrated my desire once again to end my life. There are so many things I now want to do – no, have to do: I have to see Esther and talk to her again, I have to find out what's in Kato's storage cylinder, I have to escape the Harvest, I have to live. But my time is almost up. It's unfair. My phone rings and I grab at it, hoping it's Esther but it isn't, it's Ken. How did I forget about him? In my desperation to contact Esther, Kato or Minamoto, I must have completely blotted him out of my mind somehow, but I'm glad to see his face. He's calling to find out whether or not I've heard anything yet about Esther, and when I tell him I haven't, he tells me he's heading to her apartment just in case she's been sent back there. For just a moment, I consider abandoning my own plan and heading to Esther's place myself, but there's no point in both of us going there. If she's home, Ken will call me and I'll head over straight away, perhaps even with Kato's storage cylinder. I tell Ken where I'm going and he wishes me good luck but there's something in his voice. It's hard to properly describe his tone, but I'd say it's like when someone is saying "farewell" without actually wanting to say "farewell".

Like many of the streets in the city centre, the Kettei Building coffee shop is virtually empty. It's an eerie sight, like the aftermath of a cataclysm in a movie, but the cataclysm hasn't yet arrived. It's on its way. Most people are at home now with family or close friends, saying their goodbyes and wishing each other peaceful new lives – but not me, and not the solitary staff member behind the coffee shop counter. She's stacking saucers on a shelf and seems to recognise me by her bright smile as I walk over to her, but she doesn't say anything.

"I've been told you have a storage cylinder for me," I say, hopeful that she really does have a storage cylinder for me.

"Can you tell me your name, please," says the woman.

I stop and think for longer than I should. I hope it doesn't look suspect. "Michael Tamura," I almost growl, just managing to remember which name Kato said he'd leave with the staff. Even without him being present, he's still able to make me angry.

The woman reaches under the counter and hands me a brown storage cylinder with a misted outer casing. Most everyday storage cylinders look the same but this particular one feels familiar, even down to the name 'MICHAEL TAMURA' printed in large blue letters along the side. I can't think why. "Here you go, Mr. Tamura. Happy Harvest Day." She smiles and resumes stacking saucers.

The cylinder is weighty. "What time did the man bring this in?" I ask.

She stops stacking and says, "About five minutes ago. He only just left."

"Which way did he go?" I make no attempt to disguise the urgency of my question, but she looks surprised that I even asked.

"I don't know," she says. "He just went out. Maybe you passed him without noticing."

Before she finishes speaking, I race out into the street to look for him, but even as I'm pushing through the doors, I'm remembering last night and Kato's disappearing feat. I stand on the pavement alone; he's nowhere to be seen. I return to the coffee shop counter, annoyed but not at all surprised that he's vanished again, and I angrily pull the lid off the cylinder. What I see inside shocks me and I almost drop the misted brown case on the floor. I can't take out the contents in front of the woman, I have to go somewhere private, so I run to the toilet and close myself in a cubicle. I open the cylinder again and very carefully pull out a handgun. Is this Kato's idea of 'finding a way out'? I've truly never hated a man as much as I hate him right now. There's a slip of paper inside the cylinder too, which I accidentally scrunch up in anger before I have a chance to look at it properly. Opening the thin strip again, I read: 'THE GUN IS LOADED. GO TO THE ROOF'. I check to be absolutely certain there's nothing else inside the cylinder, even dipping my hand inside and feeling around. I think I'm hoping to find another slip of paper telling me this is all a joke and nothing is really as bad as it seems, but the cylinder is empty. Everything is as bad as it seems. I push the paper into my pocket and I think about putting the gun back into the cylinder and returning it to the counter, but despite my terrible experience with guns, I have a horrible feeling I'll need to take it with me if I'm going to learn what Kato's up to. I hate him even more now. I tuck the gun into the back of my jeans, making sure my T-shirt is hanging far enough below my waist to conceal the weapon completely, and I run out of the coffee shop into the building's main lobby. The woman behind the counter shouts "Thank you" and "Goodbye" after me, at which point I remember I've left the storage cylinder in the toilet cubicle. 'It doesn't matter,' I tell myself, 'It's empty.'

A security guard is dutifully standing in the centre of the empty lobby area. As I run to the elevator, he holds up his hand and calls out, "Sorry, no one's allowed up today. The offices are closed."

"I have to go up! It's important!" I protest.

"Sorry, sir, you'll have to come back tomorrow."

"Please, you don't understand!"

"I can't let you go up there, sir, I'm sorry. Come back tomorrow."

I feel my hand twitch toward the gun hidden in the back of my jeans. I have to get to the roof, it's as simple as that, and there's no way I'm going to be stopped by an unarmed security guard. But will I actually pull out the weapon and threaten him? Have I become so terribly desperate, so far removed from the man I used to be, that I'll resort to such an awful thing? Maybe I have. Surely nothing I do now can possibly make matters any worse? I resist. I'm not that man. Yes, I'm desperate, but I'm not that man. 'I hope I'm not that man.' "Look, you have to let me go up there! Please!" I have to persuade him somehow. Perhaps if I tell him I work here and I've left some important thing on the top floor that it's vital I pick up before the Harvest Light arrives, he might believe me. "My name's Michael Tamura, I'm…"

"Ah!" The guard suddenly smiles as though he knows me, or at least as though he's heard good things about someone with the name Michael Tamura. "You're Michael Tamura then?" He seems to relax. "Sorry to have held you up, sir." He pushes the button to open the elevator doors and bows as I step inside. "Have a good day," he says. As the doors close, he adds, "And Happy Harvest Day."

'What the hell…?' I'm certain Kato is getting some kind of pleasure out of making me 'play the role' of Michael Tamura. I don't know what he's doing, what his ridiculous scheme is, but as the elevator climbs the forty-nine storeys to the top floor, the thought that I'm trapped in his cruel plan makes me angrier and angrier. But I'm concerned even more by the fact that in my desperation, I almost pulled a gun on the security guard. Did Kato known this might happen? Did he endanger an innocent man for the sake of whatever twisted game he's playing?

Eventually, the elevator arrives at the forty-ninth floor and I leap out before the doors are even halfway open. Sprinting past section after section of dark and ghostly deserted workstations, I follow the highlighted trail of emergency indicators to the roof exit and I'm soon at a small flight of stairs leading up to an exterior door. Already out of breath, I race up the steps and push the door open, and I'm almost blinded by an explosion of dazzling sunshine. But my mind is instantly taken off any potential damage to my sight by the slight but noticeable vibration I now feel beneath my feet and the low hum I can hear, surely louder than it should be at this stage. My eyes are hurting, still trying to adjust to the shock of the intense sunlight, but I look behind me, past the sloped, hut-like exit I've just burst through, and to my horror, all I can see is the great amber wall moving slowly toward the building. Every structure, every road, everything in existence over a kilometre-or-so east of the Kettei Building is already on the other side of the Light! How could my initial guess of one and a half hours' grace have been so catastrophically wrong? I probably have ten minutes left, if that.

It's already far too much for me to try and cope with all that's happening, to handle my crime, my attempts to escape, Esther's kidnap, virtually everyone's disappearance, Kato's taunting, but now I also have to fight my own debilitating fear. I see the Harvest Light so unbearably close now and my natural inclination is to freeze, to give in and submit to the inevitable, but now isn't the time to surrender to my usual startled paralysis; now is the only time I have left if I'm to do anything – and I have to do something. I'm up here for a reason: Kato has told me to come; I need to find out why; I need to find Esther. I turn away from the approaching amber wall to the west end of the building and see, next to the perimeter barrier, a smartly dressed man sitting on a large case. I can't make out his face clearly yet but I already know that it's Kato. Even if I weren't partly expecting to find him up here anyway, there's just something about the way he's set himself so nonchalantly on the case that tells me I should hate him. This time I have no hesitation in grabbing the gun from the back of my jeans – this man is not innocent – and I run at him. "What the hell are you doing?" I roar. "Where's Esther?"

Kato remains seated until I'm only around five metres away from him. As I get closer, I realise he's smiling. "That's the spirit, Mr. Machida," he calls out, and stands up. "Straight into action!" He calmly tucks his hand into his jacket and pulls out a gun and points it at me. There's no chance to try and battle my fear this time; I freeze instantly. I don't mean to, I don't want to, but despite the fact that I'm both furious and armed, this world of weapons and intrigue simply isn't my world. I'm still terrified. My own gun is pointed in Kato's general direction but my hand is shaking. If either of us decides to pull the trigger, I know I'll be the only one to get shot.

"I'm curious," Kato says, taking his seat on the case again. "Did you threaten the security guard?"

I'm fuming inside – 'He knew that was going to happen!' – but I won't satisfy his curiosity. "What do you want, Kato? Why are you doing this? Where's Esther?"

"This 'straight to the point' you is much better than the old indecisive you. It'll certainly make life more interesting," he grins. "So, what do I want then? You. Simple as that. Why am I doing this?" He seems to think for a moment. "Just in case; to cover my bases, if you like. And where's Esther? She's in this case."

My stomach turns. What has this madman done to her?

"Y'know," he continues, "If you concentrate hard enough, you can probably shoot me from there and not hit the case. What is it, five metres, five-and-a-half? Do you want to try?"

'What the hell is he doing?' "What have you done? Is Esther still alive?" I almost choke on the question.

Kato sighs. "She could be. But if you don't hurry up and shoot, you're never going to find out. The Harvest Light's coming."

"Why do you want me to shoot you? If you're so keen to die, just shoot yourself and get the hell out of my way!"

Kato seems to get a little annoyed. "Come on, Mr. Machida. Don't start hesitating now. Look, I'll make it easier for you. If you don't shoot me by the time I count to three, I'll shoot you. One…"

My heart is pounding so heavily it's giving additional wobble to my already quivering gun hand. Adding to this, the tremendous gusts of wind at forty-nine storeys which would, on any other occasion, be mercifully cooling, but right now they're only shaking me off balance, there's no way I can make a straight shot even if I want to. "Please, just tell me why you're doing this!"

"… Two…"

I'm a civil servant! I sit in an air-conditioned office every day processing births, deaths and marriages, and to most of the world, I might as well not exist! How am I in this situation again, armed with a gun, my life in the balance? I have to act, I'm trying to aim, but I don't think I have it in me to actually shoot him in cold blood. But I need to help Esther! "Please, Kato, tell me why you want me to do this!"

"… Three."

25

In Memory of A Killer.

The trigger feels ice cold against my fingertip. I'm not applying any pressure, my finger is locked tight, but there's such an unnatural sharpness of contrast from the freezing strip of metal to the burning hot air on either side of it, I can make out the trigger's shape exactly. It's quite wide at the top and tapers just slightly to a more ergonomic width at the point where its user will pull hardest. There are also two tiny grooves set just a couple of millimetres in from the edges of the trigger, following its smooth curve from top to bottom. This could be for flamboyant design but I suspect it aids in increasing grip. I'm sure Nishi's gun didn't feel like this.

I haven't fired. But neither has Kato. It's almost like we're frozen in the moment, like time has stopped on this roof, and I'm suddenly aware of the terrified expression that must be fixed to my face now. In contrast, Kato is looking very angry indeed. He's also no longer looking at me. And now I see why.

"He's doing this because he got worried," Minamoto calls out, walking toward us from the direction of another roof access door.

"For crying out loud, Minamoto!" Kato shouts. "You're like a bad smell!"

"I guess that explains why I hang around you," Minamoto retorts. He turns to me. "Put the gun down, Machida. He isn't going to shoot you."

"Did you take classes in how to spoil other people's fun?" Kato hisses. He turns his gun away from me to Minamoto but I keep my own gun pointed toward him.

Minamoto doesn't seem to care that his life is now in danger too. "Seriously, Machida," he says, "Put your gun down."

Although I haven't fired and although I still don't feel like I can, I now find I can't turn my gun away from Kato. My arm is stretched forward, it sways left and right, up and down, all around my target, reluctant or unable to centre, but powerless to let him go. I don't know if it's anger or fear keeping the weapon trained toward him but either way, I don't feel completely in control of my actions and it's frightening. What's happening to me?

"Anyway," Kato growls, "I'm not worried."

"Wait!" I cry out. "What's he worried about? Why's he doing this?" I'm asking Minamoto but I can't take my eyes off Kato, even though he's no longer pointing his gun at me.

"He got worried that you might be starting to listen to Esther. And to me," Minamoto replies.

'You haven't told me anything useful!' "Listen to you? About what?"

"About the Harvest. Esther said she had a hope that the Harvest Light would be merciful: that it wouldn't punish you for your mistakes. Remember, I hinted at the same thing. You were starting to think seriously about that and that's what Kato's worried about."

"Why is he worried about that?" It's only after I've asked the question that I realise Minamoto has just said things he can't possibly have known about. "Wait, how do you know what Esther said to me? How the hell did you know I was starting to believe her? Who the hell are you?" I suddenly find myself pointing my gun at Minamoto too. *'What's going on here?'*

"Oh, this is interesting!" Kato cheers and lowers his own gun. "Shoot him instead. I don't mind."

Minamoto raises his hands in half-hearted surrender. "Really, Machida, you should put the gun down. I'm not joking."

"And what makes you think I am!" I cry. "Oh, that's right, you can somehow read my mind, yeah?" I think I'm starting to lose what little grip I have on this whole situation. Who is this man really? Who are these people? I'm scared, but not of them; my confusion and my anger are violently reacting against one another inside me, they're producing irrationality, a heightened potential for unpredictability unheard of in Nicholas Machida or Michael Tamura, and my capacity to contain these erratic, volatile natures is crumbling faster than I can patch it together. I can feel the two grooves in the trigger steadying my grip, ensuring my finger doesn't slip off the thin, death-delivering metal strip, and I know that in the next few minutes I could very well kill one of these two men. I don't want to do it, I'm trying not to, but I still can't make myself lower the gun.

"No, you've got it wrong," says Minamoto, "of course I can't read your mind. I'm just linked to your Rice Grain, the same way Kato is."

I'm not certain I've heard Minamoto correctly. The roof of the building is vibrating even stronger now, the sound of the Harvest Light is growing louder as it draws nearer, my brain is having quite some trouble keeping my wits in place. "Did you say, 'linked to my Rice Grain'? What do you mean? Have you been spying on me?"

"Your whole life," Kato chuckles.

"No, it's not like that, don't listen to him," Minamoto says. "What would you say if I told you Kato and I are Harvest Agents?"

I glance back and forth between the two men: a 'civil servant' and a 'salesman'. Harvest Agents are myths, creations in fantastical and sometimes frightening stories parents tell to their children to make them behave. Minamoto and Kato obviously have great resources, they're obviously not of the professions they've claimed to be, I'll grant them those things, but they're not imps. "I'd tell you to stop wasting my time!" I shout.

"Trust me, I'm not wasting your time," Minamoto presses. "What would you say?"

I don't know why I'm answering him. "I'd say you're crazy! Both of you!"

Kato interrupts, "Crazy? That's an old one. But it's tough luck, I'm afraid. We're not crazy. And at the moment, neither are you."

Minamoto continues, "I know where you're coming from, Machida, seriously I do. And you're kind of right, in a way: the type of Harvest Agents you're thinking of are just weird characters in old stories. And I've never liked that description anyway, it sounds too sinister – and a little made-up. The proper word is *Intercessors*. But whatever you call us, we are real. And because we're part of the Harvest, we're linked to your Rice Grain the same way the Harvest Light is. Everything your Grain records, everything the Light reads, it's all here." He taps his forehead.

"And here," Kato says, tapping his own temple.

"Liars!" I scream. "Stop trying to mess with my mind!" My head is pounding, I'm becoming dizzy with the stress, and I can feel my finger increasing pressure on the trigger.

"I don't think you're doing so well, Minamoto," Kato chuckles to his alleged counterpart.

"Look, Machida," Minamoto sighs, "How else would I know that you want to put the gun down but you can't, and the thing you're most scared about right now is accidentally killing me or Kato? How would I know that you're wishing you went to the toilet when you had the chance, or the real reason you shaved yesterday is because you didn't want to give Michael Tamura a beard before you had all five ID layers on, so that he could essentially decide for himself?"

He's correct on all four counts – and am I really as insane as I sound about Tamura and the beard? This is almost too much for me to take on board: that these two men, an acquaintance and a colleague I've come to know in the past four days by what I thought was mere coincidence, are in reality somehow unlike average people: that instead they're part of an ages-old system, familiar yet completely alien, and way beyond my comprehension. I'm not sure what to say but it doesn't seem to matter, the words just spill out anyway. "Who… what? I don't understand. I don't understand how any of this can be happening."

Minamoto smiles a little. "You don't really have to understand how or why it's happening, Machida. Actually, I'm not sure that's even possible. You just have to accept that it is happening." He lowers his hands despite the fact that I'm still pointing the gun at him. "Look, this is the way it all works," he continues. "The Harvest doesn't come around every seven years to see whether or not you've been a good boy; people have just started believing that kind of thing over time, but it's simply not true. The Harvest and the Rice Grain were designed from the beginning to assess the subconscious. That's the criteria for going to Euchaea. That's all it's ever been. Doing good things, not committing crimes, all of that, they're the intended by-products of applying a good subconscious but they're not the deciding factors for whether or not somebody goes to Euchaea. Over the years, all of these customs and rules people have built up around the Harvest have just blurred it's actual aim: to accept people for Euchaea who are suitable on the inside."

Kato interjects with some sarcasm, "Yeah, but tradition is so much fun!"

Minamoto shoots him an angry look.

"But what about what I did?" I stutter. "What about Nishi?"

Minamoto turns back to me. "Sure, you shouldn't have killed Nishi and you certainly shouldn't have tried to get away with it. But I've been watching you racing around trying to fix things you can't fix and escape from things you can't escape from, and you're wasting your time. You're focusing on the wrong thing. Yes, Nishi's death needs to be paid for, that's the simple truth, but your focus should be on your attitude to what you did, not just on the action of what you did and how you might get away with it. And you can't get away with it, by the way."

"My attitude? My attitude is *I'm sorry*! I'm so sorry any of this happened! I'm sorry I decided to walk to work, I'm sorry I met Nishi, I'm sorry I killed him! It was an accident! I really didn't mean to do it!"

Kato smiles. "Actually, you did. Just in that moment before you pulled the trigger. It was him or you, and you decided it was going to be him."

"That was just instinct. I was protecting myself. I wasn't out to murder him."

"Why didn't you shoot him in the arm?" Kato presses. "If you didn't subconsciously want to kill him, your instinct would have had you shoot him there."

"I – I don't know, it was just a reflex!"

"A reflex that would have had you shoot him in the arm, sufficiently incapacitating him, if that's what you'd really wanted. Remember, Mr. Machida, I'm linked to your Rice Grain: everything you do, everything you think, everything you feel. The simple fact is, you killed him and you wanted to do it."

The actual incident, the shooting of Mr. Nishi, is something of a blur now: heightened emotions, a gun, blood, and guilt are pretty much all that remain. But Kato is right: it really was 'him or me'. I made a choice in that moment. I decided to kill him. As the awful realisation dawns on me, after all of my protestations and self-pity and cries of innocence, which now seem to be all-out lies, any remaining self-worth very soon vanishes. I lower the gun. I'm a murderer.

"That's enough, Kato!" snaps Minamoto. "Machida, nobody's one hundred per cent innocent. Okay, so not everybody kills someone, but you all feel and do bad things. It's in your nature. But if it were left like that, there'd be no one in Euchaea at all and no purpose for this city. That's why there are Intercessors. We intercede, and physically step in if need be. And trust me, there's a serious need here!"

I can hardly speak. The truth of who and what I am, despite Minamoto's lenient exposition of our human condition, is still tearing at my insides. What does it matter about humanity's capacity for good and evil? So what if nobody's one hundred per cent innocent? I still took someone else's life because I chose to. I'm still a murderer. "So what am I supposed to do? I can't change anything now. I didn't mean – I thought I didn't mean to kill him, but I did. I'm guilty!"

"Well, the first thing you should do is *put that gun down*!" Minamoto yells.

There's no point to anything now. I drop the weapon on the ground.

Kato cries out, "Why'd you make him drop the gun? What's wrong with you?" but I try to ignore him, as does Minamoto.

"Next," Minamoto continues, "You need to hand your crime over to me."

I don't understand. "What?"

"Balance of justice. Crime still needs to be paid for, it doesn't just go away. You need to give me the responsibility for what you've done."

"What? Blame you? I can't blame you for Nishi's death!"

"You're not blaming me. There's no doubt that you did it, you're just handing over the guilt and the punishment. It still needs to be paid for and I'll pay for it. That's what I've come here for. And you don't have much time left, Machida!" Amazingly, I've stopped registering the approach of the Harvest Light but it's so close now. The buildings I could see less than kilometre away are all beyond the Light, all part of another world now, post-event, but the amber wall is almost upon us. I have just a few minutes.

"But if you take the punishment, what happens to you?" I shout over the increasing noise of the Light.

"Exactly what should happen; justice is done. Don't worry, it'll be sorted out. But we don't have long left!"

'Exactly what should happen; justice is done'? What's that supposed to mean? This is madness. I barely know what to say. "Well how do I hand it over to you?"

"You just do it," says Minamoto, gently. "And remember, I'll know if you really have."

There's that same sincerity again in Minamoto's face, the one that I saw when he was first introduced at the DBDM. It's inviting and honest and it's still a little surprising, but this time it's tinged with urgency due to the colossal oncoming wall of light. I think I trust him. I don't feel comfortable blaming him for Nishi's death, it's not the right or honourable thing to do, but I try to remember what he said: I'm not blaming him; I fully accept that I did it, that I'm guilty, that I deserve the punishment. But I'm passing on my condemnation for the crime. Minamoto is willingly taking over my guilt so that I can go to Euchaea. It doesn't feel right doing this; he doesn't deserve to pay my penalty. But he declared, *'I'll pay for it. That's what I've come here for'*. He actually said those words. Is there really such a system in place, such an astonishing, incredible hidden element to the Harvest: an Intercessor to pay for others' guilt to allow them into Euchaea? I don't understand it but it seems there is. I think what Minamoto said may be right: fully understanding the Harvest may not even be possible. Perhaps the Harvest really is merciful after all. I have to believe so if I'm going to do this properly. What a day. "Okay," I find myself saying. I'm smiling: I never expected to be smiling today. "It's yours."

Minamoto smiles back. "Thank you, Machida."

"No. Thank you." I mean it more than I've ever meant anything in my entire life. I feel the pressure and the burden, the unbearable and previously inescapable pain of my guilt, suddenly lift off me like a physical load. It's amazing. The feeling is so definite, so clear and tangible, I can almost picture Minamoto taking the torment away from me and I almost leap into the air with elation. Although I don't fully understand how, or even why, the impossible has happened; I've been rescued from The Terror! I'm free, I have a future, I have a beautiful life to look forward to! Now I'm ready for my Harvest. Now I'm not scared. I bow in the deepest of gratitude and shout again to this most amazing man, "Thank you!"

"Well done, Machida," winks Minamoto. "You've done it. You've given up your guilt. Now don't try to take it back, and don't go doing things to take on any more, okay. You're going to be a citizen of Euchaea now."

"Don't worry, I won't," I holler, wiping the tears from my eyes. I didn't even know I'd been crying, but I think they're tears of happiness this time so I don't mind them, just like I don't mind still being a little puzzled. *'Don't try to take it back? Why on Earth would I want to do that?'*

26
Kettei.

I've forgotten all about Kato. As he stands up, I can see he's extremely annoyed, and I remember the case he's been sitting on with Esther allegedly inside. How can I possibly have forgotten? Have I been so overwhelmed by stress and now happiness that I'm not able to focus anymore? That's no excuse. I truly must be falling apart.

"See, I knew all of this would happen," Kato moans, "Which is why I brought our special guest." Keeping his gun trained on me, he unlocks the case and with some effort, pulls out a very limp body. It's Esther.

My stomach turns again – *'No! What has he done to her?'* – but as I'm about to scream that very question, she suddenly snaps into life, flailing her arms, trying to pull away from him. I'm so relieved she's alive and conscious, I think I smile again for a moment. She's clearly shaken but thankfully, at least from this initial glance, I can't see any evidence of physical harm.

I immediately start toward her but Kato pulls her to her feet and presses the barrel of his gun to the side of her head. "Just wait a second," he says. "Esther's got something to tell you, haven't you, Esther?"

"I thought you and Minamoto were Intercessors?" I cry out. "What the hell are you doing, Kato?"

"Come on, Mr. Machida, surely you don't need this one explaining to you too?" Minamoto says. "Not all Intercessors come from Euchaea."

I have no idea how or why it's taken this long for me to realise where Kato is actually from. Maybe I've been blinded by fear or anger or even by the hope he's been offering me – up until last night, that is. But as I suddenly realise what's going on, that this other Intercessor is here on behalf of The Terror, I'm filled with dread. Minamoto has come to help me; Kato has come specifically to do the opposite. And now he's holding a gun to Esther's head. I have to do something. "What do you want?" I ask him, already terrified of whatever answer he might give.

Kato smiles. "You've already asked me that question, and the answer was 'you'. Remember? So let me answer another question instead: why did I bring you up here? Well, you know I like to cover my bases and that means being prepared for any eventuality, like Minamoto taking responsibility for your guilt. But Nishi's death still needs to be paid for; it's not going to just go away. Contrary to what you might think, Mr. Machida, I'm a subtle man so I didn't want to do *this* in the street." Before any of us can react, he quickly moves his gun away from Esther's head, shoots Minamoto in the chest, and turns the gun back to Esther.

It all happens in an instant, yet somehow it all seems to unfold in slow motion. I see the hanging cuff of Kato's suit jacket trail slightly after his wrist as he extends his arm away from Esther to Minamoto and I watch it sway in the air as he steadies his aim. The kickback of the firearm coincides almost exactly with the explosive bang of the shot and Minamoto's chest seems to burst open. He lifts off the ground as though hit by an invisible car, and lands on his back, his arms limp at his sides. And after this, three of us are suddenly back in the exact same position we were in less than a second ago.

I can't believe what's just happened; I feel paralysed. Esther is absolutely terror-stricken. Her eyes are shot so wide it looks like they might pop out of their sockets at any moment; she seems to be trying to scream but no sound is coming out of her open mouth.

The feeling returns to my legs and I run over to the wounded man. It looks bad, it looks very bad, but I think he's still alive.

"Punishment isn't pretty," Kato sighs, composed. "No one ever realises just how bad it's going to be until it actually happens. It's a bit sad really. I don't think I'll ever get used to it." And suddenly he's smiling again. "But let's not get too sidetracked. Come on, Esther, what were you going to tell him? Harvest's nearly here and then it'll be too late."

My terrified friend stares straight at me, but there's something else there, aside from her fear at being held at gunpoint. She looks almost guilty. "Nick, I'm –." She struggles with her words. "I'm a Harvestee. This is my Harvest too."

I go completely numb. I can no longer hear the tremendous hum of the Harvest Light nor feel the vibration in the building nor even see the man holding the gun to my friend's head. Now I understand why Esther was starting to question the plan and why she was so concerned about 'deliberately helping me to commit a crime' by using the Rice Grain wrap. Now Esther is guilty. She knowingly condemned herself in order to help me.

What has she done? What have I done? My senses return. "Esther, no! You can't be a Harvestee! Why didn't you tell me?" I cry.

"I'm sorry!" Tears are streaming down her face. "At first, it was supposed to be a surprise. I was going to surprise you and Naomi in Euchaea. But then all of this happened and I couldn't tell you. You wouldn't have let me help you if you'd known. You probably would've gone back to trying to kill yourself instead. I couldn't let you do that."

"No, Esther! You shouldn't have condemned yourself for me!"

Kato calmly interrupts, "And there's the dilemma. But all isn't lost. Well, not for all of us. Minamoto kindly explained about taking on other people's guilt, so I have a suggestion: take on Esther's guilt. Now that you're not carrying your own guilt, you're considered innocent and therefore able to take on hers. If you do that, she doesn't get condemned for helping you. Of course, it means you'll come with me, but at least she gets to go to Euchaea."

"No, Nick!" Esther cries. "Don't do it!" But there's no question about it. She should never have been put in this situation in the first place; it's my fault that any of us are here now and I'll do whatever I have to do to help her, even if it means forfeiting my own place in Euchaea. The only thing worse than going to The Terror is watching my friend go there because of me.

"Don't, Esther," I tell her, sternly. "You're going to Euchaea. I'm not letting you go to The Terror!"

"That's right, Mr. Machida," Kato beams.

"Don't listen to him!" says a voice barely audible above the ground-shaking sound of the Harvest. The Light is now right on us and breaches the perimeter barrier of the Kettei building roof. The incredible droning is now so deep, so loud, even the air itself is vibrating. We have seconds left.

Minamoto lifts himself onto his elbow and tries to sit up. "He's lying!"

"I gave you a chance to say your piece," Kato hisses, "Now it's my turn so please shut up!" He turns his gun on Minamoto again but this time, before he can shoot, Esther grabs his arm, trying to fight the weapon away from him. She claws and writhes like a wild animal but he's much stronger than her – the struggle won't last. As quickly as I can, I leap into the tussle and punch Kato in the face as hard as possible, allowing Esther to twist the gun free. Instinctively, she turns it on him.

"Don't shoot him!" I cry out, already fearing I'm too late.

"No, shoot!" says Esther's intended victim. "Think about it: if you let Mr. Machida shoot, there's no innocent person to pay for your guilt and you'll both be coming with me. If you shoot, then he stays innocent and only one of you has to go to The Terror. You can even decide whether or not to give your guilt to him, so it'll be up to you who goes. Either way, it's the best deal you're going to get today."

Esther is trembling. I can only imagine the sheer rage she feels toward him. He's kidnapped her, threatened her life, and now she's pointing a loaded gun at him with the ideal opportunity not only to get revenge but also to save her friend from The Terror. There's no time to talk her out of it. I throw myself at her, grabbing her hands and forcing the gun barrel toward the ground. "Don't do it." I say this as calmly as I can, though in my mind, I'm screaming frantically. "It's okay, Esther. Look, the Harvest's here. As long as you're going to Euchaea, I'll be okay."

Esther sobs, "I can't, Nick."

"Yes you can." I'm amazed at how calm I suddenly feel consoling her; maybe it's because I know this is the right thing to do. "You can even tell Naomi I was really heroic." I chuckle. I never expected to chuckle.

"What the hell's the matter with you two?" Kato cries out, "Don't any of you have the guts to shoot? I guess it's a good job I always come prepared." He lifts the back of his jacket and pulls out an extra gun, immediately training it on Esther and I.

There's no time for us to react, no time to think of defending ourselves or ducking down, just a bang. And Kato falls to the floor.

"I said he's lying," Minamoto says, quickly shuffling toward us with his own gun drawn, conscious of the Harvest Light catching up behind him. "Doesn't anybody listen? Your Rice Grain is your own, and everything on it, including your guilt, is your own: other citizens can't take your guilt away from you, all of you are the same. Only Intercessors can do it. Kato's just manipulating you. That's the way he works." He coughs. It looks painful. "And he wasn't really trying to help you postpone your Harvest either, Machida. He knew I might convince you to hand over what you'd done so he just wanted you to keep on looking for a way to escape. That way, you'd hold on to your guilt. Anything and everything he could do so that you end up going with him."

Immobile on the ground, Kato twists his head to look up at Minamoto. "Have I ever told you how much I hate you?" he growls.

Minamoto looks back at him. "Yes." He kicks the gun away.

My head feels like it's about to burst with questions that I can't answer and I imagine Esther probably feels the same but we're very nearly out of time and Esther is still condemned. "But if I can't take Esther's guilt, what happens to her?" I plead.

"The first thing that happens," Minamoto shouts above the Harvest noise, "is that you put that gun down! Kato isn't going to shoot you, either of you. He just wants one of you to shoot him."

"What? What the hell for?" cries Esther, dropping the gun.

"If either one of you shoots him, it'll be a deliberate act. You'll be condemning yourself. That's all he wants. It doesn't really matter which of you does it, as long as he can take at least one of you back with him."

Kato laughs out loud on the floor, obviously in pain too, "Sorry, Mr. Machida. I guess you weren't really so special after all. But if it's any consolation, I wanted both of you."

I try to ignore him. "So what about Esther? The Light's here!"

"I know what you've done too, Esther," Minamoto says. "But you were right, the Harvest is merciful. I know you were trying to help because you cared, so the same thing goes for you as it did for Machida. Give your guilt to me."

Esther bursts into tears again. There's no time to spend thinking about it, wondering whether or not Minamoto can really take on her guilt too, but she doesn't seem to need the time. She seems to know he's genuine. It reminds me of how far I've come and of how far I've yet to go if I'm ever to master the gut reaction. "Thank you!" she says. "Thank you so much!"

"Not a problem," Minamoto says, coughing up some blood as the Harvest Light reaches his back. He grimaces, wipes his mouth, and smiles a little. "See you later." The awesome amber light completely envelops him, and for a second his whole body seems to glow – and he's gone.

"Hey, Mr. Machida, Esther," Kato calls out. We turn to him. "Just so that you know," he says, also smiling, "you were this close."

Neither of us says a word, neither of us can. It really was *that* close. We can only hold on to each other as the Harvest Light approaches. I feel Esther's arms clamping around me, tighter and tighter as the Light draws nearer;

she's shaking – maybe I am too – and she looks at me, wide-eyed, as if to say, *'This is it!'*

I think my expression back says, *'Here we go!'* or *'It's going to be fine!'* or *'I'm sorry for everything I've put you through. I can be such an idiot!'* but at the corner of my anxious, dry, open mouth, I can feel a definite smile, and I can tell she's seen it too. And within a second, we're inside the Harvest Light. It's warm here; it's not like the blazing heat of the sun we've been enduring on the exposed rooftop: this is a comfortable warmth, a temperature perfectly tuned to my body. Maybe it's perfectly tuned to Esther's body too. Although I've just left the burning sensation of the roof, this feels like stepping into a heated room direct from a cold street; like I've completely submerged myself in a soothing hot bath; the sensation of relief is instant.

I suddenly remember that in all of my other Harvests, the Light has never felt warm to me before.

I'm falling.

27
Processing.

At least I think I'm falling. Or maybe I'm weightless. My stomach doesn't feel like it's where it should be, I'm being spun around and around by a strong wind, or by the air pushing past me as I hurtle toward… something. I don't remember the point at which I closed my eyes. It might have been when I started to fall – or when I became weightless. I don't remember at what stage the tremendous droning of the Harvest suddenly vanished either. Now I can't hear a thing except my own shallow breathing. I can't even hear the wind rushing by me. My legs won't move. It's because I'm standing on something solid. Did I land? I didn't feel an impact. Was I falling or floating at all?

I open my eyes and I can see nothing but dazzling amber light. It's nothing like the yellow-orange tint of my bedroom that frightened me so much just hours ago. Now I realise that was the very poorest of comparisons. This is the real thing, intensely brighter, inexpressibly sharper, glorious instead of terrifying. I have to squint, to almost shut my eyes completely, in order to make anything out, but what I can eventually see still isn't much: my hands are only just coming into focus when I hold them up in front of me, there's a faint dark line where a floor becomes a wall, a far fainter line about two metres above me where a wall becomes a ceiling. I'm in a room – an empty one, it seems – still bathed in the amber Harvest Light, my whole body tingling. And I'm still feeling that soothing warmth. Perhaps this is what it feels like to be teleported. I blink a few times in rapid succession to try and assist my eyes in adjusting to the light; soon I can see the ceiling and walls and the floor a little clearer but there's no detail to pick out, they're completely blank. And there's no Esther. "Esther! Where are you?" I shout out with a surprising and altogether confusing combination of mild panic and simple curiosity. Before I have time to start analysing whether I'm concerned for her safety or just wondering where she might have strolled off to, someone coughs behind me and I turn around to see Minamoto sitting on the floor. His gunshot wound appears to have worsened drastically and his shirt is now drenched in blood. If I don't do something quickly, he's going to die; but I'm in an empty room in some mystery place I don't know; there isn't much I can do. I run over to him and he looks up at me, smiling.

"Machida," he wheezes, "What can I do for you?"

"*What can you do for me?*" What a question to ask. "Nothing! You need to get to a hospital!" I crouch down and steady him. For the moment, I don't know what else to do.

Minamoto holds on to me as I try to keep him propped up under my arm. "No, I don't need a hospital," he says. "What did I tell you before: Trust me, everything'll be sorted out. In a few days, I'll be right as rain."

"But you're in agony," I feebly say.

"I've been shot in the chest," he replies, dryly. "Yes, I'm in agony. Will you just trust me."

This is all too strange. He's ignoring the wound, trying to have a normal conversation as though nothing's wrong. I can't concentrate. But I suppose this is Minamoto's territory; this is the world of Intercessors and of staggering exonerations and of Harvest technology and procedures no one in the city I've left behind will ever understand. I should trust him like I did before, trust that he knows what he's talking about, despite the fact that, to me, it clearly looks as though he's bleeding to death. I'm going to have to try very hard.

Suddenly I remember Esther. "Where's Esther? What happened to her?"

Minamoto seems to have been waiting for this question. "Don't worry," he says. "She's fine. She's here too. Everyone arrives in his or her own room like this. You'll see her soon, and everyone else."

I'm instantly relieved to hear that she's okay: it seems my emotion was a little more mild panic than simple curiosity after all. But it's still hard to know what to think, or what to say. "Okay. She's alright. That's good. So then… what happens now?"

Minamoto's head dips a little. "The light's fading," he struggles to say.

"You have to hold on!" I cry.

"No, I mean the amber light around you is fading."

Now I'm embarrassed.

Minamoto continues. "Soon it'll disappear and so will I. When that happens, you'll know what to do and where to go. Remember, trust me. But before that, I believe you have a question."

"A question?" I'm not sure what Minamoto means. I'll know what to do? I'll know where to go? Is this room really inside the Harvest Light? There must be billions of questions, relevant and completely irrelevant, firing in my mind right now; I can't think which one he's talking about. "I'm sorry, you've lost me. Again."

"You want to know why you and Naomi were called seven years apart."

How can I have forgotten about this too? Every day for seven whole years, this question has bothered me, and on the morning of the incident with Mr. Nishi, I'd been especially determined to ask it. The last four days have clearly pushed the question clean out of my mind. And besides, in all honesty, I don't think I ever seriously expected to be given an answer anyway.

"It's simple enough," says Minamoto. "Seven years ago, you weren't ready. Now you are. The names aren't chosen at random."

'The names aren't chosen at random'. Is he saying there's yet more hidden design to this already astonishing system? That not only is the Harvest Light assessing the Rice Grain for something else entirely, that not only are there measures in place to try and rescue those doomed to The Terror (and, unfortunately, counter-rescue measures too), that it isn't just a straight-forward, colossal, random filter, but that the people selected are selected for a reason? What reason? That we're *ready*? How do we know when we're ready? And now another startling realisation hits me. "Do you mean that if I was called seven years ago, when I actually wanted to be, I wouldn't have come to Euchaea?" I'm stunned: I feel a little like I've narrowly missed being hit by a train – which, in some way, I guess I have.

"Probably," Minamoto smiles. "It's not really for me to say."

I can hardly believe it. Thirty-four years and I haven't really understood the Harvest at all. "Was Nishi ready?"

"What you think of as 'ready' and what's *really* ready are two different things. Yes, Nishi was ready. But he gave up, he didn't want my help."

"I'm not sure I understand," I tell him, and it's true. I don't think I can take onboard anything more today. The combined mental, emotional and physical stress has been unbelievable, truly more than I could bear, and yet somehow here I am at the end of it – I'm going to Euchaea. Through the incredible act of someone else, someone I've barely known, I'm alive and I'm well and I'm soon to see the people I love and miss. Just a few days ago, I wouldn't have dared imagine this.

"Don't worry," says Minamoto. "You'll get it in time. It always takes a while but you'll understand eventually."

I now notice how much the amber light has thinned all around me. I'm propping Minamoto up with my left arm but I can almost see my hand through his body, as though he's becoming transparent, fading with the amber. It shocks me so much that I almost drop him. "What's happening?" I almost panic.

"It's nearly time now, Machida," Minamoto rasps. "Off you go. I'm sure there are people out there who can't wait to see you."

His words cause a giant, almost involuntary smile. Those people's faces are already in my mind: Naomi, Esther, my parents – this is unbelievable! I'm ready to see them; I'm becoming almost overwhelmed with excitement and emotion now, but I'm ready. "Thank you, Minamoto," I say. "I really mean that." Crouched as I am, I bow deeply still. It feels in some way inadequate, but it's all I can do.

"I know," he smiles again. "I'll see you in a few days."

Minamoto and the amber light are disappearing, becoming fainter as though slowly being concealed by fog, and as they recede, the true brightness of the room is being revealed. It's like the walls, the floor and the ceiling are made of purest white light: I can barely see, but I can hear a low hum somewhere far away. I think it's the fading sound of the Harvest. It will take a moment for my eyes to adjust again, but even before that happens, I can already feel a wonderful sensation, a kind of buzz, simultaneously spreading from my Rice Grain, from my stomach, even from my hands and my feet, consuming my whole body. I've never felt this before but the experience is amazing.

I can make out the shape of a door in the wall in front of me; I don't know if it's always been there or if it just appeared – it wouldn't surprise me now if it had just appeared. Either way, the incredible euphoria I'm now feeling makes me think I could almost float toward it. But maybe I'll walk instead. Or perhaps I'll run. It's time to go.

Printed in Great Britain
by Amazon